AMONGST THE MAR

1

"What do you expect to find when we get to Mars?" asked Dmitri Ivanov. The Russian's merry green eyes scrutinised his American colleague's face with intense interest as he waited for a reply.

Josh Walters thought for a while and then shrugged his broad strong shoulders. His deep black eyes showed mild surprise at this question from his Russian friend. It was a question he had often asked before of every other crew member and Josh was puzzled as to why he was asking it again. When Josh asked why he was asking, the Russian became quiet and his green eyes took on a distant look as if a great stream of thought was passing through his mind. After a moment he looked back at his American friend and Commander and said that he was interested in finding out if almost ten months in a spacecraft, surrounded by nothing except an infinite expanse of space, had changed his perceptions and thoughts.

"Well, I certainly feel a lot more humble," Josh replied, "Whenever I look out through the windows I realise how puny and insignificant we humans are when compared to the sheer vastness of space. Yet on earth we all strut around like self-important peacocks who believe the whole universe revolves around us. Now I realise the universe couldn't care less. Even if our planet was obliterated why should the universe care? After all, it's got billions of others to occupy itself with, and I'm damned sure many of them contain civilisations a lot more advanced and enlightened than ours!"

"In that respect I feel exactly the same way as you do," the Russian replied thoughtfully, "however, I'm more interested in hearing your thoughts about Mars. Do you really expect to find the remains of an alien civilisation? Has your new-found sense of spiritual wonderment at the glory of the universe made you feel any different about the prospects of discovering signs of an extra terrestrial culture? I mean, half the people on Earth probably expect and wish that we do. This controversy has raged ever since the Viking mission sent back those pictures of the so called Face and the other enigmatic structures, and very soon now we will finally have a chance to discover the truth."

"Let's wait until we get there, shall we," Josh replied. "I like to keep an open mind on matters and I don't want to build up any unrealistic expectations only to have them dashed later on. As far as I'm concerned, being part of the first manned expedition to the red planet is achievement enough. To stand on the surface of Mars will be a dream come true. The very fact that we have got this far, the fact that we are now only three thousand miles away from the planet itself, is achievement enough. Let's take it one step at a time."

"What about you my dear Ilya? What do you expect to find?" Dmitri turned and asked his other colleague and fellow compatriot who sat at the same table drinking coffee. "Have your perceptions changed? Are you too daunted and humbled by the infinite majesty of space?"

"I am fully aware of the dimensions of the universe!" Ilya exclaimed. "It fills with me with no special awe. Besides, it doesn't look very friendly anyway. Rather than being in awe of it, I am more in fear of it and its terrifying indifference and hostile silence. As far as Mars is concerned, I expect to find a dead, lifeless and frozen planet. That's all. This is my last space mission. After twenty years orbiting in space stations and flying to the moon one begins to get tired of space travel. In fact the more I travel in space the more I appreciate the comforts of home. Let's face it... there won't be any restaurants or cinemas where we're going. There won't be any ice hockey games or unlimited reams of literature to entertain us, will there? Don't get me wrong... I'm just as excited as anybody else on this mission to be here. I'm looking forward to being on Mars. But I can tell you now... when it's all over I'm looking forward to a well earned retirement. This will definitely be my last space mission."

"I hope I never become as cynical as you! I for one expect to find marvellous things on Mars," Kevin Tanaka declared excitedly. "I don't for a moment believe those strange looking structures photographed by the Viking missions, especially the Face, are the products of natural erosion. I am certain they are alien artefacts. Those images have haunted me since childhood and drove me to become an astronaut. I for one believe we will make a fantastic discovery. I am so excited I can hardly contain myself for joy."

"Yes, I tend to agree with Kevin," Lorna Kelly declared with quiet confidence. This declaration of support from Lorna, for whom Kevin long had a soft spot, brought a wide smile to his face. He beamed at the pretty blonde astronaut as she continued... "My gut feeling is that life did once exist on Mars. A life form advanced enough to erect sophisticated architectural monuments. I firmly believe that's what we'll find."

"Hah! You Americans are so gullible," Dmitri retorted good naturedly. "You're so quick to believe in anything that sounds weird and outlandish. Your souls have not been tempered by centuries of suffering as ours have been. We Russians have always been more practical and down to earth."

"I think you're generalising again, Dmitri," Josh answered. "I didn't say I expected to find any alien monuments on Mars. I only said that I like to keep an open mind. I can assure you plenty of Americans have had their fair share of suffering too. Furthermore, don't forget it was your country that collapsed fifty years ago after more than seventy years of communism."

"I knew I could trust you to bring up that small detail again," Dmitri replied.

The voice of Natasha Molotov came over the loudspeaker. It announced that Mars was now in view and that everyone must return to their stations in the control room. All the people seated around the white table in the observation lounge leapt to their feet and rushed to their positions. The doors of the control room slid open to reveal a stunningly beautiful view of Mars through the large window at the front of the spacecraft. They found the other five members of the crew riveted to the breathtaking panorama that lay in front of them.

"Just look at that view. It's simply awesome!" exclaimed Lee as the others walked in. "We're here at last! Just this view makes the whole trip worthwhile."

Against the desolate pitch-black backdrop glistening with far distant stars, the glowing orange world was a lovely sight to behold. After an arduous ten month journey hurtling through the lonely vacuum of endless space, the crew of the spacecraft Ares had arrived. The joint American–Russian crew had passed the time deeply immersed in each other's company. Whenever they looked out through the windows of their craft and saw the stark yet hideously beautiful expanse of infinity that surrounded them, it made them realise how alone they really were. That made their relationship to each other become that much more important and stronger. They held conversations that lasted for hours on all kinds of topics. For the Russians the favourite topic was the near miraculous turn around of their economy and how they had managed to catch up with America so quickly. The Americans, however, were keen to point out the still considerable advantages they possessed as a nation. Nevertheless, when they arrived at the planet both were dumbstruck by the beauty of the sight that met them.

The glowing orange globe capped and footed with white polar caps emitted its radiance into the blackness that so completely enveloped it, as a lighthouse would light up the darkest night. The cratered, faulted, undulating topography was stunning. The network of channels that scarred the planet surface was so reminiscent of dried up river beds that one was compelled to accept that at one time mighty rivers coursed through it. The gigantic volcanoes that lay scattered around on the surface were even more stunning. The predominant orange hue of the planet contrasted dramatically with the dark brown patches that covered the surface and the strikingly white polar caps. The radiant aura of the planet was in stark contrast to the two moons that orbited it. They were lifeless dark grey stone objects that exceeded even the Earth's own Moon in their deathly pallor.

"It's even more beautiful when you see it in real life!" exclaimed Josh Walters. "I thought all these years of watching photographs and computer enhanced images of Mars would have prepared me for this. I've seen hundreds of them. Yet here I stand, totally mesmerised by the glorious sight in front of me."

"I echo your sentiments exactly," said Lorna Kelly. "In its own way it's just as wonderful as looking at Earth from space. Mars with its harsh orange beauty and Earth with its gentler blue effervescent loveliness. One complements the other perfectly. The other planets of our solar system must all be equally wondrous to behold in their own unique ways."

"Can you imagine what it must be like to watch Jupiter from such close quarters!" exclaimed Kevin Tanaka. "I mean can you really imagine what it would be like to be in close proximity to a planet that is hundreds of times larger than Earth? At least Mars is roughly the same size as our world. The sheer size of Jupiter would almost demolish the human mind! That really would be something."

"One step at a time Kevin," Josh replied half jokingly. "For the moment let's just admire this world. This in itself is a momentous historic occasion and it's only right that we give it its due respect and solemnity."

"Kevin! That's not quite correct!" Lorna exclaimed affectionately. "Mars is almost the same size as Earth only when you compare the respective landmasses of the two planets. Don't forget that all the water from the former seas of Mars has evaporated. Thus the actual land surface area of Mars is roughly the same size as the combined continental land mass of Earth. However, when you take into account the huge surface area of Earth that is covered by our oceans, an amazing seventy five per cent, then our world is much much larger. In actual fact, Mars is only a quarter the size of Earth!"

"Show off!" Kevin responded with a joyous twinkle in his eyes.

"The atmosphere is so thin as to be virtually non-existent," Natasha declared excitedly. "I can almost see the surface of the planet even from this distance. The Valles Marineris is absolutely fantastic! It looks like a gigantic scar upon the face of the planet, and just look at the size of those volcanoes! If Earth didn't have plate tectonics our volcanoes would have been just as big. Thank God they're not!"

"Look over there!" Kevin shouted. "That has just got to be Olympus Mons! Now that's what I call a volcano! It's such a shame that the time constraints of this mission won't allow us to visit it and study it. I would dearly have loved to have seen it from close quarters. After all, it's not every day one gets a chance to see a volcano that's fifteen miles high."

"I'm afraid Olympus Mons will have to wait for a later mission," Josh answered. "We have to focus our attention on the Cydonia region. Since we will have only seven days on the surface of Mars it's more important for us to concentrate our resources on one specific area and learn as much about it as we possibly can. This mission just doesn't have the time or resources to mount a planet wide exploration and study. I'm sure in due course a better equipped mission will do that and if you're still so keen, Kevin, you can volunteer to return."

The first six hours were spent in orbiting the planet. The sophisticated cameras and scanners scoured the planetary surface, extracting every bit of information they possibly could. For the most part the pictures did not reveal anything that they did not know already. The hundreds of images coming through from the surface showed the rusty orange wilderness pock-marked with craters and covered with rocks with which every schoolchild on Earth was familiar. Yet the natural features of Mars provided a sumptuous feast for the eyes despite their desolate surroundings.

The volcanoes were larger than Mt Everest and some of the canyons stretched for thousands of miles. The mountain ranges were taller and more extensive than the Himalayas and the Andes put together. The dried up river beds and seas and lakes were bigger than anything on earth. This was even more incredible when one recalled that Mars was much smaller than Earth. The temperature readings confirmed the coldness of the world they were about to enter. At the poles the temperature stood at minus two hundred degrees Fahrenheit. At the Equator it hovered around the minus forty degrees Fahrenheit mark. The astronauts fervently hoped the Martian Conditioning Process proved effective. Otherwise the mission would be a non-starter, and considering all the expense, effort and time it took for them all to get here that really would be a shame.

"The Martian region of Cydonia is directly below us," Dmitri Ivanov called out as he sat at the navigation console. The blue screen of the navigation computer had yellow grid lines on it and within each grid red and green lights flashed at random intervals. "I have locked the Ares into a stationary orbit. The distance to the surface stands at exactly 1005 kilometres. The weak gravitational force of the planet is exerting only a minimal pull that does not pose any threat to us. Our cameras are not powerful enough to determine the authenticity of the structures located in Cydonia from this distance. We will have to wait until we get into the shuttle and fly in closer to the surface before we can see clearly enough. Anyhow, it won't be long now before we all have our questions and doubts answered once and for all. I am looking forward to it."

"You're not the only one," said Lee. "From this distance all the objects below us look like nothing but rocks, boulders and hills. The terrain is simply littered with them. I sure hope that our so-called enigmas don't turn out to be nothing more than rocks and boulders."

"A planet-wide scan reveals no indication of any organic life," Mary Morgan stated quietly. She sat in front of a multi-screen console which was bedecked with intermittently glowing pink and green lights. The console with the red screen recorded the levels of planetary radiation. The green screen provided a meteorological survey of the planet, and the black screen showed the results of the organic life survey. "Owing to the thinness of the atmosphere the level of ultraviolet radiation from space bombarding the surface is immense. However our thermal suits and the Mars Pigment will protect us well enough. The Martian Conditioning Process, if it works as it should, will prepare us admirably for the harsh atmospheric and planetary conditions we will encounter. Dust storms will be a common feature upon the surface. If you look to the right you can see one currently in process. However I am picking up one unusual reading for which I have no scientific explanation. There appears to be a source of pulsating energy within the Cydonia region exactly thirty kilometres from our designated landing spot. It is located deep below the surface in a mountainous region bordered by a gigantic plain. I cannot determine the exact nature of the energy source. It's possible it could be caused by natural Martian phenomena such as geothermal activity."

"Dmitri, any ideas as to what it might be?" Josh asked.

"It is electromagnetic in nature," Dmitri replied, "It's more than likely it is connected to the electromagnetism of the planetary poles. Or it could be just an underground deposit of magnetic iron ore. Don't forget, this is Mars, and its famously unique orange coloration comes from the abundance of iron oxide in the soil. Any more than that I cannot say. We will have to wait until we get to the surface to find out more."

"Okay, I've noted down the coordinates and we'll check it out when we get to the surface after we've finished our primary task in Cydonia," Josh replied. "Melicia will stay behind onboard the Ares. She will transmit the data we send to her directly to Earth in a continuous ongoing process. In addition to that, if there is an emergency while we are on the planet surface it is good to have at least one person who has the chance to escape with all the newly amassed data or be able to render assistance in some manner. The rest of us will travel down to the surface and start our explorations of Cydonia. The space shuttle is ready for launch and once we have completed the Martian Conditioning Process we shall depart immediately. I know we are all very excited and want to start exploring straight away."

"Now at long last we will be able to discover the truth about those enigmatic objects sighted in Cydonia," Josh declared loudly. "Now we shall see if Russian scepticism wins out against so-called American gullibility."

"I hope you're not including me in that band of Russian scepticism and cynicism," Natasha exclaimed. "I have never expressed an opinion one way or the other on this matter. Don't let the hard-nosed realism of my fellow countrymen on this mission blind you to the fact that we Russians were studying psychic phenomena long before your famous X-Files appeared on television. Have you forgotten that I was especially chosen for my psychic sensitivity? The Russian soul has always been sensitive to the world of the spirit. Even seventy years of communism could not make a dent in that. Have you forgotten how religion and many new age spiritual paths blossomed in my country after the collapse of communism?"

"Of course not, Natasha," Josh replied with a broad grin. "Forgive me for my careless remarks. I didn't really mean anything by them, as I'm sure you're aware. It's just my light-hearted way of getting back at Dmitri and Ilya. They take things so seriously! Anyhow, let's all go to the conversion chamber to undergo the conditioning process."

"I really hope this process works," Kevin Tanaka said as they walked through the white metallic corridor which led to the conversion chamber. The portholes the astronauts walked past revealed a clear view of the moon Phobos. It's dark cratered surface looked foreboding in the extreme. "It would be a shame if we got to the surface and then immediately dropped dead owing to hypothermia."

"Hah! That would be sad," Ilya laughed out. "However, I have full confidence in the process. Don't forget it was thoroughly tested on Earth by locking people away in refrigerated compartments where the temperatures reached minus three hundred degrees Fahrenheit. In no place on Mars do the temperatures even get close to that. Besides, we'll be spending our time in fairly close proximity to the equator, where the temperature rarely falls below minus eighty degrees Fahrenheit. Indeed, in the summer season temperatures at the Martian Equator can often climb above zero."

Yuri, who was walking immediately behind the two men, laughed. He told them that the process was tested on him by sending him into the depths of Siberia, where he lived in a specially constructed compound with absolutely no heating of any kind. Part of the testing process was that he live there totally nude. This process was also repeated on the island of Severnaya Zemlya in the Russian Arctic. He told them the process worked perfectly and that he was not in the least bit worried about its ability to be adapted to Martian conditions.

"Let's hope you're right, Yuri," said Kevin, "but don't forget it's a lot colder on Mars and there is not the added complication of there being virtually no atmosphere, not to mention the extremely high levels of ultraviolet radiation. Oh well! I guess it's a case of 'in God we trust'. I'm glad to be here, no matter what."

The eight astronauts walked into a room which held ten transparent cubicles. Each stripped off and got into one of them and pressed the orange button on the console located within each cubicle. The cubicles sealed up and filled with a purple gas which totally hid the occupants from view. This gas was altering the human physiology so that it could live on the surface of Mars without the need for cumbersome space suits. Their internal body heat was raised to offset the bitter coldness of Mars. The red blood cell count in each body was multiplied five hundred fold to maximise oxygen utilisation. Their skins were coated with an extremely thin transparent coating of the Mars Pigment which acted as a shield against the ultraviolet radiation. Their lungs were modified so that they could process the thin carbon dioxide atmosphere. After ten minutes the gas cleared and the cubicles reopened. The astronauts walked out and put on their special thermal suits. These dark blue boiler suits gave additional protection against the harsh elements of Martian nature. They were now ready to descend.

The astronauts felt a slight sense of disorientation and mild nausea, but they knew that was a side effect of the process and would soon pass. They walked to the shuttle-craft bay and entered the blue craft. Strapping themselves into the chairs in the cockpit, they started their pre-flight checks and safety procedures. Everything was in good working order and the vessel started to emit the familiar droning sound as the engines fired up. Josh asked Melicia to seal the shuttle bay and open the external hatch. As the hatch slowly lifted the planet loomed up in front of the shuttle's viewscreen. Josh pressed the ignition button and the craft shot forward. The last thing they heard as they left the Ares was Melicia's voice over the communication console wishing them good luck.

2

One of the primary purposes of this mission was to establish the true nature of the enigmatic objects sighted in the Cydonia region by earlier explorer missions: primarily the so-called Face on Mars and the pyramid shaped structures photographed by the Viking missions in the 1970s. Heated controversy had raged on Earth for years about these objects. In one camp were those who stridently stated that these objects were the signs of an alien civilisation on Mars. Another camp refused to believe that these structures might have been artificially created, preferring to believe they were simply the products of natural erosion.

As the shuttle travelled through space the view through the small circular side windows was eerie. Even after ten months the astronauts had not yet quite got used to seeing space whenever they looked out. The sheer extent of the blackness around them made them feel humble. The familiarity and relative safeness of travelling on Earth had been replaced by a dimension of infinite strangeness. Although they were all thrilled to be here and looked forward to being on Mars there was always an element of nervousness and trepidation which hovered around the rims of their minds and it was only the fierce resolve of their courage and arduous training that kept that fear at bay. Out here one could not afford the idle luxury of fear.

"Now at long last we'll get a chance to see the so-called Face at first hand," Ilya spoke out. "I've always maintained that it's nothing more than a piece of rock weathered by the dust storms over the centuries into a structure that resembles a face. It is only a bizarre freakish natural feature. All this talk about it being an alien sculpture is a load of nonsense."

"I wouldn't be too sure, Ilya," Lorna replied. "I've studied that picture a thousand times. The more I look at it the more convinced I am that it is a face of a Martian entity. Besides, it's not only the face that we've come here to study. The Viking Missions also photographed other strange looking features, including things that look like pyramids, a pit in the ground and skyscrapers. I for one will reserve final judgement until we actually see them close up. It won't be long now!"

"Look!" Kevin shouted excitedly. "The view is incredible!"

The sight that greeted them as they neared the surface was more breathtaking than any one of them could ever have imagined. The mighty chasms they flew over stretched for thousands of miles and looked like bottomless pits leading straight to the depths of hell. The volcanoes were frighteningly huge and made Mount Everest look like a sand castle. Craters littered the place. Some were only a few meters wide while others were several hundred kilometres in width. Many of the craters had deep layers of white frost within them which sent a shudder through the astronauts' spines. They fervently hoped that their thermal suits and altered physiology would protect them against the bitter alien cold that awaited them.

"Take a close look at that area over to the right of us," Kevin said. He was looking intently at something, as if something unusual had caught his attention and he wasn't quite sure what to make of it.

"I see them, Kevin!" Mary Morgan responded enthusiastically. "They don't appear to be natural features at all!"

The closer they got to their destination the more they could see what lay beneath them. The more clearly they saw the greater their excitement rose. Strange structures caught their attention. For amongst the natural rock debris that littered the surface, in between the craters and surface fractures, were structures that stood out like a sore thumb upon a hand. Structures that looked undeniably unnatural. Structures which simply had to be the handiwork of applied alien intelligence.

"Oh my God," exclaimed Lorna, "that really is a pyramid! It's not a huge boulder or a hill at all! It's a pyramid!... It's sides are far too smooth and geometrical for it to be a natural feature! Just look at the sheer size of it! It makes the great pyramid at Giza look like a child's toy. It must be at least a mile high!"

"Look over to your east!" shouted Natasha Molotov excitedly. "There's another pyramid even bigger than this one. It must be at least two miles high. This is all the proof we need that an advanced civilisation once existed here. I can't wait to get to the surface. This is the most exciting discovery in the history of the world and we are directly involved with it. It's wonderful!"

Natasha could hardly contain her sense of jubilation and excitement. Kevin and Lorna too were ecstatic. Their cries and excited remarks filled the shuttle cockpit. The normally staid Russian men had looks on their faces which indicated that they were greatly surprised even though they managed to contain their excitement very well. The shuttle circled the top of the larger pyramid and saw at close hand its smooth uniform consistency of construction. They were somewhat daunted by its huge dimensions. There was no doubt now in anyone's mind that what they were seeing was an artificially created structure. Undoubtedly, the passage of time had taken its toll and it looked worn and battered but it was still undeniably an artificially created structure that shocked all those who saw it.

"Look over to your right," Kevin called out. "What are those things over there? They look like skyscrapers. I can see six of them. They don't have any windows or doors. They're simply gigantic slabs of rock. Very bizarre."

"I shall switch the shuttle to gliding mode and perform an initial aerial survey," said Dmitri.

"What do you say now, Ilya?" Kevin shouted excitedly. "Do you still believe they are the products of erosion?"

"It looks as if I've been proven wrong," Ilya replied with a gaping mouth as he intently observed the structures below them. "At least I will be able to end my career on a high note. I can return home and tell my children and grandchildren that I discovered the remains of an extra terrestrial civilisation on Mars. They will be extremely proud."

The sight below them was truly mesmerising. The implications and ramifications of this discovery were staggering. It proved that life once existed on Mars, life intelligent enough to have constructed such impressive and imposing pieces of architecture. This was the first piece of real evidence that humans were not the only inhabitants of the solar system. When the people on Earth received the news about this discovery it would unleash hysteria of epic proportions.

"I can see the headlines on Earth's newspapers even now!" Lorna shouted wildly. "'Ancient Monuments Discovered on Mars.' We are witnessing history in the making and I am so thrilled and happy to be such an important part of it. This moment will undoubtedly go down as one of the major turning points in human history. The first human contact with the remains of an actual alien culture. At least that we know of."

The sight of pyramids and strange looking tower blocks caused great excitement. To discover the signs of intelligent life in an otherwise dead and uninhabited planet thrilled the senses and fired the imagination. Yet the sight also produced conflicting thoughts and emotions. What had happened to the builders of these structures? Were they truly dead or could they still be around in some form? These buildings were undeniably alien yet they looked familiar. Had the astronauts travelled so far across space, to an alien planet that was supposed to be so very different from their own, only to see objects they could easily see back home? After all, the cities of Earth were full of skyscrapers and the pyramids of Egypt were renowned throughout the world. So what were they doing here on Mars?

"There's one thing that puzzles me," Lee Golding mused out loud. "How come there are pyramids here and on Earth? Sure, they're a lot larger than Earth's pyramids, but they are of the same basic construction. Did we come all this way only to see things we can see back home? How is it that two planets separated by millions of miles, with no cultural links that we know of, possess similar types of architecture? It's weird!"

"There are more things in heaven and earth than are dreamt of in your philosophy, Horatio," replied Lorna, trying her best to sound philosophical. "That's one of the questions we will try to answer while we're here. Maybe there was a link at one time. Perhaps people like Daniken are not such cranks after all. What if there is truth in their statements that Earth was visited by aliens in the past? Could it not be possible that it was these aliens who brought the blueprints for such structures to Earth and all that the Egyptians and Greeks did was copy them? Let's keep an open mind for the time being. At this particular moment I am the most excited and bewildered person alive."

"You're not the only one," said Josh, trying to maintain the cool sense of composure for which he was so admired. Yet it was clear to all that he too was tremendously excited by what he saw.

As the craft travelled slowly over the area the view below became steadily more transfixing. The pyramids were the first objects to be clearly identified. The intriguing collection of tall structures that Kevin had noticed were located a short distance from the larger pyramid. A close-up zoom showed them to be gigantic stone monoliths with the tallest one standing at two thousand feet high. The greatest excitement was caused when a large object was sighted directly behind the skyscrapers. For there on the ground clearly visible for all to see was a gigantic face. It was the famous Face on Mars that had been seen by millions on earth via the well-known controversial photograph. It was a humanoid face and to see it now with their very own eyes still had the power to shock their minds into stunned awe.

"At long last! There it is: The Face of Mars!" shouted Kevin Tanaka. "It really is a face! It's got eyes, a mouth with teeth, lips and a forehead. It's the face of some Martian who used to live here! Just wait till the people back on Earth get a load of all this. It is just simply mind blowing."

Actually seeing the Face with their own eyes stunned everyone. They had all seen the pictures but seeing it first hand was a completely different experience. Back on earth there was always the element of doubt to contend with. One wanted to believe that it really was a sculpture carved out by Martians but the mind had a tendency to dismiss it as a freakish product of natural processes. But now there was no room for doubt.

"Well, Ilya, what do you say now?" Lorna exclaimed.

"It certainly does look like a real face sculpture," Ilya replied in a surprised and subdued tone of voice.

"Are you seeing what we're seeing, Melicia?" asked Kevin.

"Perfectly," came the reply over the communication console. "I'm almost at a loss for words. The shuttle cameras are transmitting the pictures back just fine. I'm just as stunned and awe-struck as the rest of you. I don't really know what to say at the moment. It's like being in a dream. I am recording and compiling every single iota of data you're sending back."

"Oh, this is no dream," exclaimed Kevin. "We'll keep you informed of developments."

"Fine. I am transmitting the pictures directly back to Earth as they're coming in," said Melicia. "It will be at least a week before Space HQ receive the data and can start studying it. They are going to be over the moon!"

The shuttle closed in on the ground and at a height of five hundred feet Josh called out for everyone to prepare for touchdown. By this time the sight below them was crystal clear. For the most part they saw a barren rusty orange world that looked particularly cold and unwelcoming, but the presence of the enigmatic alien structures imparted an aura of feverish excitement that seemed to envelop the whole area in an irresistibly beckoning invisible warm glow.

A gentle thud indicated that the craft had landed.

"We've landed," Josh called out. "It's nice and warm inside this shuttle but outside is a very different story. The external temperature reading stands at minus eighty degrees Fahrenheit. I don't think even our Russian friends ever had to contend with temperatures like that in Siberia. Let's hope these suits and the conditioning process are working okay. Get ready, I'm going to open the doors now."

The crew braced themselves by wrapping their arms around their bodies and huddling close to the person they were sitting next to. The doors opened out upon a rusty orange plain. The sudden rush of bitter cold struck them painfully. It felt like an attack of extreme frostbite which froze every cell in their body. Fortunately it lasted only a few seconds and the Martian Conditioning Process kicked into action almost immediately. Soon they felt okay. Whilst they could not say the cold they felt was comfortable it was at least bearable. If it had not been for the conditioning process they would have died of extreme cold within five minutes.

They emerged slowly to look at their surroundings. The sky overhead was pink in colour and extremely thin, affording a view of twinkling stars even though it was still daylight. The environment they found themselves in was harsh and barren: an infertile rusty orange wilderness, littered with rocks and pock marked with craters. Yet the presence of the alien monuments that surrounded them made everyone forget the reality of their surroundings, at least for a while.

The face was huge. It towered above them to a height of over a mile, making them feel like ants standing beneath an elephant. The side profile clearly revealed a nose, ears and a strong jutting jaw. One got the impression that the person depicted was a being of enormous power and resolve. The gigantic reddish orange sculpture blended perfectly into the terrain it lay in and contrasted dramatically with the pink backdrop of sky behind it. To the side of the face stood the skyscrapers: dull brown buildings that looked like gigantic, monstrous and soulless silos. Behind them were the two pyramids. The environment around them was still and lifeless. They were all struck by how quiet the surface of Mars was. It was an eerie silence that made the spine tingle. The astronauts felt as if they were standing in a massive planetary mausoleum. Up ahead one could see the sun through the thin pink sky. On Mars the sun was like a pale yellow fuzzy orb, half the size it looked from Earth. It gave the impression of being a star much depleted of its energy.

"We've finally made it to the surface of Mars!" Dmitri declared triumphantly.

"We have indeed," Josh responded with equal pride. "How does it feel, Dmitri?"

"Wonderful. I am experiencing excitement, pride and great joy all at the same time," the Russian replied. He was surveying the surrounding terrain with avid interest even though, apart from the monuments, there was nothing of real interest to see. It was simply the fact of being upon an alien planet that imparted the aura of almost uncontainable excitement.

"Funnily enough, it doesn't feel that much different from standing on the frozen tundra of the Siberian plains," Dmitri continued thoughtfully. "Sure, the sky is of a different colour and the terrain around us is bizarre in the extreme but I have the same feeling of being in a limitless wilderness full of adventure."

"Siberia was better than this even on its worst day," Ilya suddenly said. "At least in Siberia you had trees and wildlife around you. You had deer and wolves and bears to keep you company. You could find shelter under trees and bushes which were at least living organisms. All I see here are rocks and craters. The terrain is dead and dull in the extreme. There's not even a trace of life. Even these monuments around us carry the stench of death."

"Don't be such a killjoy, Ilya!" Kevin exclaimed. "We've just made the greatest discovery in the history of mankind. Just look at those structures over there! They alone make the trip worthwhile. Just think of the fantastic new insight we will obtain about an alien culture. We've only just arrived on the surface of Mars and you're already feeling homesick for Siberia. How pathetic! Doesn't the wonder and glory of being the first humans to stand upon Mars mean anything to you? Why on earth did you volunteer for this mission if the fact of being here doesn't thrill you in the least bit?"

"Oh, I'm just as excited as you are, Kevin," Ilya brushed away Kevin's outburst. "It's just that I have a different way of showing it. One day you'll feel the way I do."

"I certainly hope not," Kevin said under his breath.

"Ilya! You're still as pig headed as ever," Natasha exclaimed with thinly disguised irritation. She looked at him in a manner which suggested that a contempt which arose from a long standing familiarity was mingling with deep rooted affection. "No wonder I decided against getting involved with you at Space Academy. Your stubbornness and almost hostile scepticism about my psychic abilities were simply too much to bear. Why can't you just be happy at discovering these fantastic ruins from an alien culture? I can hardly contain my excitement."

"I'm having a struggle mentally adjusting to the fact that I'm standing in a place which is millions of miles away from my home," Mary said. She sounded as if she was giving voice to an intense wave of mental processing that was taking place within her. "Now that we're here it doesn't feel that much different from being on Earth. Sure enough, the environment is very different. That thin transparent pink sky up there is certainly a totally new experience. The landscape and terrain around us tells me we are definitely on another planet but inside I don't feel that much different. We're still standing on soil, albeit a very different kind of soil. All around me I can see rocks and boulders and craters, again things with which I am already familiar. Now we're surrounded by alien yet once again strangely familiar structures. Within myself I'm still the same person I was when I left Earth. But I feel I shouldn't be because of the unique nature of our journey and the fact that now a vast expanse of space separates us from our homes on Earth. I guess I expected that arriving on Mars would result in some miraculous personal transformation."

"It already has! Trust me, I can see it in your aura," Natasha replied. "Don't think too much about it. Just experience it for what it is and enjoy it. Besides, I don't think it's the distance travelled that results in inner personal transformation. It's got more to do with the types of experiences that you undergo. Travelling to another planet is definitely a major consciousness altering and enhancing experience. The very fact that you're here has already changed you. Otherwise you wouldn't be thinking the thoughts that you are. We've all been transformed in more ways than we can imagine. The course of time will manifest the changes in our personalities. I mean, none of us can deny that right now we are not the same people who climbed onboard the Ares ten months ago and started this trip. The journey here changed us. Being on the planet itself has changed us even more."

"Thank you Natasha. I needed to hear that," Mary said gratefully. The words from her Russian friend helped to ease her perplexity.

"Don't worry about it, Mary," Lee added sympathetically. "If it's any consolation to you, I feel exactly the same way."

"Believe me, Mars is very different from Earth!" Yuri exclaimed enthusiastically. "You're tired, Mary. That is what's causing all these morbid thoughts to arise within you. You'll feel better after you've had some sleep."

"Everybody gather around," Josh called. "I can fully understand your enthusiasm about discovering these alien monuments but I want this operation conducted properly. Don't forget we are now on an alien planet, millions of miles from Earth. Although we like to think we know a lot about Mars, the fact is Mars probably holds more secrets than we can ever imagine. Discovering these monuments is ample testament to that. There are far too many unknown factors at play here for us to do things impulsively. Our first priority is to establish a base camp here. Then we can start studying and exploring. We shall work in teams of two and under no circumstances is anyone to venture out by themselves. I'm not taking any chances. Although there is no sign of any organic life on Mars, these structures prove that at one time there was life here. Whether that life still exists or has vanished is one of the things we have yet to establish. Until I know for sure I am going to play it safe."

It took several hours to set up the base camp. When it was complete the first shadows of night had already begun to fall. The study of the sites would have to wait until dawn. The astronauts were tired. The combination of having had their physiology altered and having to adjust physically and mentally to being upon an alien world exacted an enormous personal toll which could only be temporarily offset by the intellectual exhilaration of discovering the truncated remains of an extra terrestrial civilisation.

"Just look at that night sky will you," Natasha shouted in reverential awe.

The others looked up and gazed in silent wonder. The clearest night sky on Earth could never have afforded the stunningly crystal clear view into space that they were looking at now. The stars were bigger, brighter and seemed so much closer. The group spent a full thirty minutes gazing up at the wondrous celestial canopy that shimmered above them. It provided some consolation for the dreadful eeriness and desolation of the world they stood in, which would be their home for the next seven days. Josh turned away and headed towards the tent. The others followed. The astronauts filed into the large grey tent and zipped the entrance shut. Once inside they lay down on their mattresses and awaited the coming of sleep. In their state of physical and mental tiredness that would not be long.

"Natasha," Lee called out in a half joking manner, "you were specially chosen for your psychic sensitivity. Can you detect any Martian ghosts wandering around here?"

"No, I can't!" retorted the Russian. "There are different types of ghosts. If these Martian ghosts don't want their presence to be known then they can quite easily shield themselves against intruding minds. I would guess that the builders of these structures were a very advanced race. If their spirits are still lurking around here they could quite easily hide themselves. So in answer to your question: no, I have not detected any wandering spirits, which is not to say there aren't any. Besides I'm just too tired right now. I need to sleep and I'm sure you do as well."

"I don't believe in ghosts. This planet is well and truly dead," said Ilya. "The people who built these monuments are long gone and we've got nothing to worry about. You can take that from me."

"I wish I could be so sure," Mary Morgan whispered quietly to herself.

3

Slumber fell like a heavy comforting blanket upon the people in the tent, except for one. Mary Morgan could not sleep. She tossed and turned and was fully aware of a dust storm which raged in the distance. Its eerie howling sounded to her like the howling of wolves which she used to hear as a child living on the Canadian prairies. Only now it sounded infinitely more eerie because the wind she heard was an alien one that sounded more menacing simply because it was alien. She reflected on how strange it felt to hear an old familiar sound on an alien planet millions of miles from home.

Finally she got out of bed. Mary was not the type of person to stay in bed if sleep was not forthcoming. Since everyone else was obviously deep in the land of nod and totally oblivious to her she boldly decided to venture out, knowing full well that Josh had warned against venturing out alone. Taking a flashlamp she stepped outside into the cold frosty night. Her attention once again was almost forcibly drawn upwards to the dazzling beauty of the night sky. The stars were more numerous and much closer, and they shone with a brightness that made the heart leap with delight. Deimos and Phobos lit up the night sky as they kept their nocturnal vigil upon their planetary companion. Seen from the planet surface the glow that enveloped them made them seem less lifeless than they did from space. The stunning beauty of the celestial canopy captivated Mary's attention in a kind of hypnotic trance. An urge to wake her friends came upon her but she resisted. They probably wouldn't appreciate being rudely stirred from their slumbers, even to behold a sight as glorious and mesmerising as the one she was looking at now.

"That night sky is so utterly beautiful and awe inspiring," she murmured to herself. "I feel so much closer to the cosmos here than I ever did on Earth. At least I will be able to say to my family and friends back home that I have seen the Martian night sky in all its glory and wonder."

Turning her gaze back from the sky she looked out into the distance at the monuments. In the night they had a different ambience about them. It was similar to visiting an ancient Greek ruin in the middle of the night as she had once done. Only this time the sensation of weirdness was amplified a thousand fold due to the fact that these particular ruins were on a different planet, and pre-dated the Greek ruins by hundreds of thousands of years, at the very least. Furthermore, the sheer desolation and loneliness of the environment in which these ruins stood only added to the eeriness. The thought that her mission, all eight of them on the surface and one orbiting, were the only humans, the only living things, on a world with a diameter of just over four thousand miles inspired a sense of isolation and wary awe that she could never have imagined back home. It made her shudder nervously. The play of the nocturnal shadows made the place look a lot more eerie. At times the shadows looked like sinister figures darting around the site.

She switched on the flashlight and followed the strong beam that stretched out in front. All the while she was conscious of the howling wind in the distance and the odd swirl of dust that swept past her. The dust storm was not close enough to cause much inconvenience. Her slow careful steps brought her to stand next to the Face. The monument towered over her and she was aware of a sensation of reverence welling up within her. After all, she was standing next to a monument created by alien beings upon an alien world in the misty dawns of time. How could one not feel awe in such circumstances? The image of the Face was clear in her mind. Casting her mind back in time she tried to imagine what this world might have been like when it was inhabited by the people who built these structures. But her mind was blank. Nothing definite came to mind and she gave up this particular intellectual exercise. Passing her hand over the rock out of which the Face was made she was impressed by the smoothness of it.

"It's so incredible to be here!" Mary said to herself, "I'm actually on Mars! Oh God, it still hasn't fully sunk in yet. I'm standing on another planet millions of miles from Earth, next to a monument created by Martians in the dawn of time. Words can never express the way I'm feeling now. It feels like a dream but I know it's not a dream. This is reality!"

An urge came upon her to venture closer to the skyscrapers but she dared not stray too far from the camp. When she looked at the sinister looking structures, irrational feelings of fear and unease arose within her: feelings which she did not feel from any of the other monuments. There was something about them which caused her to become nervous and agitated and she could not understand what it was. She shrugged her shoulders and was grateful for the fact that she was within earshot of her sleeping companions, which she found comforting even though she knew she had disobeyed a direct order by being out here alone. Memories of her training for this mission wafted through her mind. The hours spent in the revolving gyroscope to condition her body to withstand extremes of gravitational pressure, the hours of arduous physical training and the countless hours spent in reading and solving complex mathematical problems. All that and much more, she had had to go through to get here. Now that she was here it all seemed strangely irrelevant. The memory of the last night she had spent with her boyfriend came to her. She wondered what he was doing and if he was missing her.

Her attention was once again drawn to the skyscrapers, and the irrational fear came upon her again. They did not look appealing in the daylight. In the night they looked positively scary. Mary tried to analyse why she felt the way she did about these particular structures. The other monuments, the pyramids and the face, held no fear for her at all and yet they were just as alien in nature as these skyscrapers. There was something about these which caused one to become nervous. She felt that they contained a dark and deadly secret. Why she should feel that way, she could not understand. Then she regained control of her morbid imagination and brushed the matter aside. She heard an extremely woeful howl and she could have sworn it came from one of the skyscrapers but it could quite as easily have been a passing gust of wind. Yet this one particular howl froze her blood with trepidation. Now she wanted to return to the tent and rejoin the security and company of her sleeping companions, and she now fully appreciated Josh's comment about not venturing out alone. That eerie howling she had heard she dismissed as being the howling of the wind and nothing more. It was then she became cognisant of a presence behind her. She knew without a doubt that there was someone behind her. Like Natasha, she too possessed a certain psychic sensitivity and knew for sure there was someone there even if she couldn't see or hear them.

Her first thought was that it must be another member of the expedition who was also experiencing a sleepless night. She called out to whoever was behind her to identify themselves. When stony silence greeted her she began to get nervous. Nobody on the expedition was of the bent of mind to play practical jokes such as creeping up stealthily behind someone. They were too mentally mature to do something like that. The silence continued and the presence remained and she became more nervous. Yet she only had herself to blame by being out here by herself. Slowly she turned around to confront what was behind her. She prayed that it might only be her imagination running off with her. She hoped that it was only a case of a passing gust of wind being mistaken for an alien presence.

When she turned around she saw a figure. It stood in the shadows and was at least seven feet tall. She could not make it out clearly except for its outline. The figure was powerfully built with long cascading hair. It said nothing but Mary sensed it was carefully studying her. Fear and terror overcame her and she became paralysed. Desperately wanting to scream for help she found that her throat had seized up and she could not utter a single sound. Her heart beat wildly and the veins in her head throbbed manically. The figure did not make any menacing movements. It seemed content simply to observe her from a distance. Then it faded away into the shadows of the Martian night.

Mary found herself alone with the Martian night again. But this encounter meant that nothing would ever be the same. They had arrived here thinking that they would be the only living beings upon an otherwise dead world. Even the discovery of the monuments had not fundamentally changed that perception because they looked so old and deserted that it was very easy, too easy, to think that they were simply the remnants of a dead civilisation that no longer existed. After all, their wonderful scientific instruments had told them there was no organic life on Mars of any kind. Now Mary felt all that had done was instil a sense of false security and confidence in them. What if this planet was teeming with other beings such as the one she had just encountered? Were they friendly or hostile? This experience had shaken her badly. Mars was not uninhabited and she had just had first hand experience of that fact, and it had terrified her out of her wits. It made her realise how woefully inadequate they were in dealing with something they knew absolutely nothing about. Suddenly this supposedly uninhabited world became full of countless imaginary terrors. This time when she opened her mouth to scream she had regained her voice and she screamed loudly and hysterically. Her screams rudely disrupted the sleep of her friends and brought them rushing out. They gathered around her slumped figure.

"What's the matter Mary? And what the hell are you doing out here?" Josh shouted.

"There was someone here!" Mary replied hysterically. "I saw a Martian. This planet is not uninhabited!"

"What did you see?" asked Dmitri anxiously.

"I'm not sure," Mary replied. "It was too dark to see clearly. But it was big and humanoid in form. It didn't say anything. It simply observed me for a while and then disappeared. That's all I can tell you."

"You had an hallucination, that's all," Ilya suggested forcibly.

"No I didn't!" exclaimed Mary, "I saw what I saw. I'm positive."

"What do you think Natasha?" asked Josh, "Can you sense anything?"

"No I can't," she replied. "Which is not to say that whatever she saw doesn't exist."

"Don't be so ridiculous!" retorted Ilya. "I'm telling you, she just had an hallucination. That's all. It is quite understandable considering the high stresses imposed upon the mind and body by space exploration. The pressure of being on Mars has finally got to her and she's cracked."

"All right, there's no point in arguing now," Josh said as he surveyed the surroundings. "Whatever it was, if it was anything at all, is gone now. We'd better get back to our tent and stay together for the rest of the night. Dmitri and Lee can stand watch tonight while the rest of us sleep, just in case. Wake us immediately if anything unusual happens."

"Being on this planet is unusual enough," Lee muttered quietly to himself.

4

Soon the team in the tent were fast asleep, leaving Dmitri and Lee alone with the Martian night. Although they wouldn't admit it the incident with Mary had shaken them. If she really did see a Martian then it meant that they were not alone. The night cast shadows upon the monuments and in their newly agitated states of mind that made the structures look even more sinister.

"This place gives me the creeps," Lee said as he drank some coffee. "I wonder what Mary saw tonight? Maybe there's thousands of them lurking around this place. What if the ghosts of the Martians who built all this are watching us right this very moment? Maybe it's the actual Martians themselves? Perhaps they never died out at all and they could still be living here? What if one of them tries to grab us tonight?"

"Relax," Dmitri replied. "Do you see any Martians now? She's just an hysterical female, that's all. Ilya guessed it perfectly, she had an hallucination. I don't think she's as mentally tough as she'd like to think she is. It's one thing to pass the training successfully for a space mission such as this, that's the easy bit. It is quite another matter altogether to contend with actual planetary conditions once you arrive. That is what really tests our mettle. Mary's obviously not up to the job since she's already cracked. Melicia should take her place here and Mary should stay on board the Ares. The stresses and strains of this mission are already getting to her. There are no Martians here. If there was even a trace of organic life here our sensors would have picked it up long before we even reached the surface. All this talk about spirits and ghosts doesn't impress me in the least. I think the Russian government should have diverted the millions of roubles they spent on psychic research into more profitable avenues."

"I'm not so sure," Lee replied thoughtfully. "I've got a bad feeling about this place. I don't know why, but those skyscrapers in particular really spook me. I just don't like them and I don't have any rational explanation for the way I feel about them. I mean, I really love those pyramids and the Face is fascinating as well, but those horrible skyscrapers: I just don't like them."

"I admit that they are rather ugly looking structures but I think you're letting your imagination run away with you," Dmitri said reassuringly. "Ilya was right. Mars is an uninhabited planet. There are no Martians or green-eyed monsters lurking in the shadows. Those monuments are as dead and lifeless as the people who built them are now. Why don't you just enjoy the scenery? Look up at the sky and marvel at its glory. Here, have some more coffee."

Both men looked up into the night sky. The thinner atmosphere afforded a clearer view into space than was ever possible on Earth. The stars shone with breathtaking clarity and they seemed to be so very close. Although by now they had seen it several times they never got tired of looking at it and marvelling at its beauty. They felt as if they could reach the stars with a single leap which, considering the much weaker force of gravity on Mars, probably wasn't too far from the truth. Only the super lead alloy in the soles of their boots prevented them from floating off into space. A pack of meteorites flew past them as they watched. The two moons were particularly riveting in their lonely grandeur as watchers over the planet. The sight of two moons in a night sky took some getting used to after a lifetime of seeing only one.

"Those moons are awesome," Lee mumbled as he poured the hot comforting liquid down his throat.

"Yes, I agree wholeheartedly," replied Dmitri. "Hey! What the hell is that?"

"Where? what?" shouted Lee, leaping to his feet in sheer terror and spilling his coffee on the ground.

Lee turned and looked at Dmitri only to find him quietly laughing to himself. It had been a practical joke. Lee breathed a sigh of relief and then started to shout angrily at Dmitri.

"Don't do that again!" Lee shouted, "You could have given me a heart attack. I don't think much of your sense of humour!"

"All right, I'm sorry. It was only a joke," Dmitri replied with a wide smirk. "Keep your voice down or you'll wake the others."

"You know my nerves are already on edge," Lee said as he calmed down somewhat. "It won't take much to push me over the edge. We don't even have any weapons with us on this mission. I'm beginning to fear that was a big mistake. What will we do if we really are confronted by hostile Martians? How on earth will we defend ourselves? Those guys at Space HQ made a big mistake in not issuing us with weapons."

"We don't have any weapons because we don't and won't need them," Dmitri said. "Besides, what use are weapons against ghosts, if that's what we're dealing with here? I apologise if I scared you. I promise I won't do it again."

The sound of the distant howling wind that had kept them company for quite a while suddenly became louder. This caused Lee to jump to his feet again in shock. Although the sound was far away it was very distinct and eerie, the loneliness of the night only adding to its eeriness. Dmitri got to his feet as well but he showed no signs of anxiety.

"Sounds like a big one," Lee said. "Hope it's not heading our way."

"We've got nothing to worry about," Dmitri replied. "The daily meteorological transmission sent to us by Melicia mentioned a dust storm but it would not affect us. We are out of its path."

"How much longer till daybreak?" Lee asked.

"Exactly four hours," replied Dmitri.

"Can't come soon enough as far as I'm concerned," Lee exclaimed as he surveyed his surroundings, "and to think I actually volunteered for this mission despite the objections of my family. I'm beginning to think I should have listened to them. Just think, I could be tucking into a huge hamburger with my kids and wife at a football game right now. Instead I find myself here on this god-forsaken refrigerator."

"You don't really mean that, Lee," Dmitri responded in a gentle encouraging tone. "You're just as excited to be here as anybody else. Deep down you're very happy to be here. It appeals to the explorer that you truly are just like the rest of us. You'll feel better when we really start exploring this place. After all, that's why we're here."

5

Meanwhile back in the tent everyone was fast asleep. Even Mary managed to fall asleep. The shock of her experience seemed to facilitate the oncoming of sleep. However, it was not an uneventful sleep. As her body lay in a state of deep slumber Mary Morgan's consciousness visited the world of dreams and experienced a series of powerful dreams which shook her to the core of her being. As her body lay sleeping her spirit wafted through regions of incredible imagery and extraordinary vividness.

She saw a lush fertile world that was reminiscent of Earth, though she knew it was not. The sky was deep pink and there were pale blue clouds. Mighty rivers and oceans of a deep purple hue mingled with large continents that contained smouldering volcanoes and majestic mountain ranges. In this first dream she saw hundreds of cities dotted all over the surface of the strange planet. They were imposing cities with marvellous architecture and she was dazzled by their beauty and spaciousness. The land masses upon which these cities were located were fertile and teeming with many different types of strange fauna and flora the likes of which she had never seen before. The cities were populated by two races of people. One was a tall powerful race with flowing red manes and purple skins. The other was equally tall but slimmer with bald heads and pale white visages that looked cruel. Yet despite the fierce appearance of the two races they seemed to live in harmony with each other and conducted all kinds of trade amongst themselves. The roads and airways of the many metropolises that she saw were filled with vehicles of many different shapes and sizes.

Then the scene changed and she found herself in totally different circumstances. A war raged on the planet between the two races. Many of the cities had been reduced to rubble. The two races fought savage wars with each other with sticks that discharged bolts of electricity and with flying chariots that shot forth deadly rays and she saw millions of corpses littering the cities and countryside. The planet had changed from a thriving civilisation to a war-torn hell. This scene caused Mary great distress and she wanted to get away from it. Then the dream scenery changed for a third time.

She dreamt she was in a bustling metropolis teeming with those beautiful people with the long red hair and purple skins. Their physiques combined raw power with grace. The men wore trouser suits which had swords that glowed with a red light attached to their waists. The women were garbed in knee length dresses and carried a similar weapon strapped to their waists. The bald race was no longer present and the previously war-torn planet seemed to have recovered. The city she was in was as wonderful as the cities she had seen in her first vision and extended for many miles. It was full of pyramids, tall skyscrapers, imposing pillared constructions, gigantic mansions and smaller oval shaped structures that served as housing for the majority of the population. There were wide open expanses of parkland that had orange grass and trees that blossomed with yellow and pink flowers. Through the centre of the city flowed a mighty river that was at least a mile in breadth. Upon this river floated boats of many sizes and shapes. Overhead she saw a flock of what at first seemed to be very large birds. Upon closer inspection they turned out to be Pterodactyl-like creatures with leathery skins. They shrieked loudly and caused fear to arise within her. Yet they caused no concern amongst the population below. For these people this flock of creatures caused no more worry than a flock of pigeons would cause on Earth.

Mary walked happily along the broad yellow pathways that sprawled through the metropolis. Although stern in appearance, the people around her did not appear to be hostile. The common form of transport seemed to be a black metallic vessel, capable of holding four people, which glided silently over black metallic pathways. The countryside surrounding the city was lush. Trees reaching up to a height of a thousand feet were common. The trees were interspersed with bushes and exotic flowering plants. The foliage was a strange mixture of green, red, purple and orange separated by wide open expanses of orange coloured savannah. Upon the savannah she saw a herd of animals that looked like a cross between an antelope and a horse. The sky overhead was of a rich pink hue with hardly any clouds.

Then suddenly a sense of deep foreboding descended upon the place. Looking up, she saw a fleet of gigantic black flying saucers appear in the sky. Their sudden appearance made the flying creatures flee in alarm. The populace became alarmed and rushed for safety. The aura of calm dignity and graceful strength which had pervaded the city vanished. Wailing sirens burst forth from all over the city. Powerful missiles from various positions within the city shot into the sky in an attempt to strike down the saucers. They simply rebounded off the craft and exploded in mid air, casting down harmful debris which burned thousands to death. An armada of attack craft hurtled into the air from bases located within the city. The vessels directed a formidable array of weaponry against the saucers. They were just as ineffective as the earlier missiles had been. One by one they were picked off by red bolts of light which shot forth from the saucers.

Then suddenly, without any warning, the saucers let loose with devastating fire-power. Massive red laser rays shot forth, incinerating everything below. Right before her very eyes she saw the city razed to the ground and the inhabitants simply vaporised out of existence. The deadly laser onslaught was followed by a pulverising with monstrous bombs that caused pillars of fire to reach into the sky. What distressed Mary the most was the realisation that this total destruction was not simply confined to this one city. No, it was a planet-wide process. The entire surface of the planet was destroyed. Every other city on the surface suffered the same fate and the countryside was not spared the same calamity. Then, as a grotesque final gesture, the atmosphere was set alight. The planet became one monstrous fireball that consumed everything within it. When the world that she saw had been reduced to a smouldering crematorium the fleet of craft swiftly retreated back into the depths of space from which they had so suddenly appeared. All Mary could do was look around in horrified bewilderment. A whole planet had been completely laid to waste in a matter of minutes.

This final dream caused Mary the most pain and anguish and she awoke screaming uncontrollably. Her cries once again rudely jolted everyone out of their sleep. They rushed to her side to comfort her. After several moments she realised that she had just had a dream and she regained her composure. She reassured them that she was fine, telling them that she had only had a nightmare and that it was nothing to worry about. When asked if Mary would like to share the dream she declined.

"I'm getting worried about you, Mary," Josh said slowly. "Perhaps you're not psychologically suited for this mission. It might be a good idea if you swapped places with Melicia. What do you think?"

"Oh come off it, Josh!" Mary exclaimed angrily. "Give me a break. I've just had the shock of encountering an alien at close quarters. No matter what any of you might think I really did see that alien. Now I've had a dream and that's no big deal. There is nothing wrong with me. If I feel I'm not up to this job then I'll tell you myself."

This outburst from Mary seemed to satisfy Josh and the others. They went back to sleep. Mary sat on her bed deep in thought. Her mind was in turmoil. For several moments she tried to make sense of everything that had happened to her. When this proved to be a futile exercise she simply released the whole thing, took a few deep breaths and went back to sleep.

6

Lee and Dmitri greeted the dawn with relief. They were tired and looked forward to getting their quota of sleep. The others emerged from the tent quickly. There was a sense of urgency about beginning the explorations. The events of the previous night added a new edge of excitement laced with a certain trepidation to the mission. Mary was a strong woman and not one prone to hysteria. The fact that she had been so badly affected by whatever she saw the previous night indicated there might be some truth in her story. At the back of their minds everyone knew this and it was making them nervous. They really hadn't come here thinking they would have to deal with intelligent life forms, of whatever type they may be. However, these astronauts knew they were going into the unknown when they volunteered and courage was an integral part of their mental profile. Mary's experiences would not be allowed to interfere in the work they had come here to do.

"How was the night?" Josh asked as he emerged from the tent.

"Fine," Dmitri replied. "Nothing untoward to report. A storm passed in the distance. Its howling was the only spooky occurrence that took place. We are both exhausted and need to sleep."

"Yes, I can see that. You look like a pair of zombies. Take as long as you need," Josh answered. "You can start your work tomorrow if you want."

The others emerged in quick succession. Ilya and Natasha wasted no time in preparing breakfast. The smell of bacon and eggs cooking on the magnetic plates wafted around the camp-site, invoking memories from Earth that were strangely comforting. It conjured up delicious images of sitting around the table with the family having a warm hearty breakfast. At least they could have some of the creature comforts from home here as well. The first destination for everyone as they emerged from the tent was always the coffee urn. The hot steaming steel vessel looked especially inviting in the icy cold environment in which the astronauts found themselves. They tended to congregate around the urn and lap up the warmth that radiated from it as they drank their coffee.

"This brings back memories," Ilya said to Natasha as he scooped up a couple of eggs from the plate, "I often used to prepare your breakfast for you back in our academy days. Don't you recall? You never liked getting up early in the morning. The air was always a bit on the chilly side first thing in the morning in that large dormitory we shared with the other cadets, and you left getting out of bed right until the last possible minute. You know something Natasha, if you hadn't been so set in your ways we could have made a good couple."

"That's rich coming from you!" Natasha answered abruptly. "If anyone can be accused of being set in their ways it's you. Being with you wasn't good for me. You never had faith in my psychic abilities. You never encouraged me in any way. On the contrary, you were constantly ridiculing me and, my dear Ilya, nothing has changed. Sure, you've mellowed out a bit but you're still the same old Ilya. Of course, I'm still very fond of you and I haven't forgotten the many good times we had together as academy fellows but, I'm glad I realised you and me would never have worked and the decision to keep our relationship platonic was a good one."

"I never realised all this psychic business meant so much to you," Ilya replied with a puzzled expression. With a warm affectionate glint in his eyes he carried on. "I really did care about you, it's just that I wasn't very good at showing it, and I still do. Oh well! It's all history now."

Mary was the last to emerge from the tent and quickly walked over to get some coffee. Everyone again asked if she was feeling okay. With obvious irritation she remarked that she didn't like them treating her with kid gloves and that she was perfectly okay, further stating that she was now even more enthusiastic about studying the ruins.

While they ate Josh began speaking.

"I am going to pair you up and allocate you to a specific area," he began. "Mary's experiences last night fully illustrated the perils of venturing out alone and I do not want a repeat performance from anyone. I don't know what happened last night but I don't want it to distract us from our mission. We've got a job to do and that is what we should focus on. Right now, looking around us, I find it hard to believe there could be any other life with us on this world. The night can often play tricks upon our senses. Everyone must work in pairs. Lee and Dmitri can work together. I will work with Natasha and Kevin, Mary can work with Ilya and Lorna with Yuri. Nobody is to work beyond the twilight hours. We are all to meet up at base camp at the end of each day to discuss our findings. In the event of an emergency all are to cease what they are doing and rush to the site of the incident. Mary and Ilya will study the pyramid structures and so will Lorna and Yuri. My team will initially study the Face and then we will make a brief study of the skyscrapers which can then be continued by Lee and Dmitri tomorrow. I think those two will be asleep all day today judging by their appearances this morning. Happy explorations everyone, and be careful!"

Breakfast was consumed swiftly and the teams paired up. Each took the necessary equipment and supplies and headed off towards their designated area. The area containing the structures was a mile square. The closest object was the Face, no more than a hundred meters from the camp. The skyscraper structures and one of the pyramids were located at the periphery and entailed several minutes of walking.

Arriving at the larger of the two pyramids Lorna and Yuri were daunted by its gigantic proportions. They had both visited the pyramids in Egypt and Mexico but this one was something totally different. One got the impression it could be the prototype for all the pyramids in the universe. Even after all these centuries of standing alone in an unfriendly uncaring world of utter loneliness and emptiness it still possessed a mysterious aura of defiance. The pyramids on Earth were constructed out of blocks of stone but this one was made out of a seemingly uniform expanse of shiny smooth obsidian type material. There were no seams or joints to indicate that it was made by putting together several different blocks. Its brownish orange bulk rose from the ground to soar imperiously into the air to a height that made its summit virtually invisible from ground level.

"It appears to be constructed out of a single block of stone. The density of the material is incredible," said Lorna. "I can't even penetrate it by one millimetre. The weight of the entire pyramid exceeds two million tonnes. If there is anything inside we're going to have a hell of a job getting to it."

"Maybe that's what the builders had in mind," replied Yuri. "What better way to hide your precious secrets and knowledge than in an impenetrable fortress. I feel certain there is something of incalculable importance within these pyramids that made the builders go to such lengths to protect it. If only we can figure out a way of getting inside. There must be a way!"

"You've certainly changed your tune Yuri!" Lorna said in surprise. "On board the Ares you were just as sceptical and cynical as Dmitri and Ilya. Now you're sounding more like Kevin and me. You're even accepting the possibility that there may be something hidden inside these pyramids."

"I can't deny the evidence of my own two eyes," Yuri replied. "I admit I was sceptical but there was an element of acting in that. It was my way of maintaining solidarity with my compatriots. After all, we go back a long way. Yet, inside, I always hoped that we would find something revolutionary on Mars. These monuments will change the way humans think about space forever. Once they see the photographs and video images that we send back, the history books of Earth will have to be rewritten. As to my comments about there being something hidden inside this pyramid, I was simply following the principles of logic. The Egyptian pyramids held the bodies and possessions of the Pharaohs. Perhaps these Martian pyramids served the same purpose? I was simply postulating possibilities."

"The thickness and hardness of these pyramid walls exceed their Earth counterparts by three thousand percent," Lorna said excitedly. "It is practically impossible for us to penetrate them with our limited resources. As to what may lie within we might have to wait for a later mission to discover. There is an interesting feature though. I'm looking at the astronomical orientation of the pyramid and guess what... it is aligned almost perfectly to the magnetic poles of the planet. Furthermore the site we are standing on is in exact alignment to the Pleiades. This information could be significant."

"Next you'll be telling me they're beacons for spacecraft!" Yuri laughed.

"Not necessarily, but it is a good idea to keep an open mind on things, don't you think?" Lorna retorted half jokingly.

"I guess so," Yuri responded. "Perhaps the terrain surrounding us might hold some clues. Let's have a close look at it. This soil has a permanent layer of frost upon it. It's a good thing our boots have excellent grips otherwise we'd be sliding about all over the place. Why are there so many rocks littering the surface of this planet? You can't walk even a metre without stepping on one of these rocks!"

"They are the remains of crashed asteroids," Lorna responded, "Which means that at one time Mars must have suffered a terrific bombardment from space. It could well be that which finished off the civilisation that was existing here at that time. The asteroids in the Asteroid Belt between Mars and Jupiter are thought, by some, to be the remains of a planet which once existed between these two worlds. It could well be that some of these asteroids managed to escape from their orbit and crashed onto Mars. When you consider that some of those asteroids are thousands of kilometres in diameter you can well imagine the kind of damage they would inflict when they impact with another planet."

"But I maintain that such an asteroid bombardment would have left behind remains and artefacts from whatever civilisation existed here." Yuri said thoughtfully. "They might be in a broken and smashed state but they would still be recognisable artefacts. The whole planet should be littered with them. Yet all we have are these isolated structures standing in an otherwise culturally dead planet."

"I can't answer that at the moment, Yuri," Lorna replied with a shrug of her shoulders.

The terrain surrounding the monument held no clues as to who might have built it. There was not a single remaining artefact or relic. There were no tell tale signs which could point towards the nature of the civilisation which had erected these enigmatic structures. No indication, either, as to why there were pyramids here on Mars and on Earth. The only feature in the landscape around the pyramid that caught their attention was a crater. The outer rim of the crater lay some hundred metres from the pyramid. When they walked to its rim they were startled by its depth. It was at least five hundred feet deep and extended for two miles in diameter. The inside of the crater was lined with a thick layer of frost.

"Only an asteroid could have made a crater as big as this one," exclaimed Lorna. "The frost layer is over a hundred meters in depth. It's probably been there for thousands of years. The temperature here hasn't risen above zero for a very long time. The ice is predominantly solidified carbon dioxide."

"If it was made by an asteroid, where's the asteroid?" Yuri said. "All I can see when I look into it is a deep layer of frost. I can't see the asteroid which is supposed to have made the crater in the first place. It suggests to me this crater was created by a different kind of impact."

"Such as?" Lorna asked with great curiosity.

"I don't know. Maybe it suffered a pulverising from cosmic rays," Yuri laughed. Lorna smiled at this humorous remark from her Russian friend. She was seeing a side of him she had never seen before. She had always believed him to be rather dour and uninteresting but she now realised she had judged him too harshly.

"The whole planet is a gigantic refrigerator," Yuri continued. "If there were any bodies of dead Martians around here they would be in an excellent state of preservation. If only we could find something tangible. These structures prove that at one time people used to live here but all trace of them has thoroughly and mysteriously disappeared. It is so frustrating. We have so many questions but right now there don't seem to be any answers. There is absolutely no sign of a source civilisation for this pyramid. One would have thought that the builders might have left behind a few tools or other artefacts!"

"Patience, Yuri," replied Lorna. "The answers will come. It could well be that the remains of the former inhabitants are buried so deep beneath the surface that we just won't be able to get to them. Don't forget our organic life sensors can't penetrate beyond five hundred metres below the surface. That means any future mission will have to come equipped with heavy digging and boring equipment. Anyway, let's try digging. It's possible there could be artefacts buried in the soil."

At the other pyramid Mary and Ilya discovered the same things as Lorna and Yuri had. The structure was constructed out of the same material and seemed equally determined to guard its secrets. It proved just as resistant to all attempts to penetrate its surface. The surface was too smooth for climbing upon and all that really could be done was to take photographs and videofilm it for posterity. This in itself was quite an achievement. They spent a couple of hours digging at several spots around the base of the pyramid. But all they got for their efforts were large mounds of useless orange earth that were full of nothing but rocks and pebbles.

It was whilst sitting down and sipping water that Mary experienced something peculiar. She was looking out at the vast plain that stretched out into the horizon to the side of the pyramid. The particular pyramid they were studying was situated at the edge of the area in which these structures stood. The cratered plain had several deep channels that ran off from it. At first she thought her eyes were playing tricks upon her. For a few seconds it looked as if the plain had suddenly filled with water and the channels were huge rivers that fed into it. She was looking at an inland sea upon which waves gently undulated. The sky up above had become thicker and she could no longer see any stars shining in it and the cloud cover had considerably thickened. Most surprising of all was the surrounding terrain. Around her she saw a lush wilderness with many forms of weird and varied flora. The pyramid was still standing where it was but it possessed a shiny lustre that was not there before. She shook her head from side to side in an attempt to clear it, doing her best to believe that this was all nothing except an optical illusion.

"Oh my God!" she exclaimed quietly to herself. "Am I really going mad? Perhaps Josh was right, I'm not suited to this mission at all."

She did her utmost to deny what she was seeing but could not. The scene in front of her looked only too real. Suddenly a tap on her shoulder jolted her back to her old surroundings. She looked up in a daze to see Ilya standing over her. He was saying something but in her state of shock she heard nothing at first. Gradually Ilya's words became audible and she regained her sense of composure. Ilya was very excited. He said that he had discovered something wonderful and that he had been shouting out to her for several minutes but she was not responding. Mary's mind reeled from her recent experience but she did not wish to say anything. Considering the events of the last few hours it might make the others doubt her mental health even more. If she told the others about what she had just seen Josh might become convinced that she really was unsuitable for the mission and send her back to the Ares, and she did not want that. She decided it was best for her to say nothing.

"Oh, I'm sorry Ilya! I was just thinking about my children back on earth," she said, trying to think up an excuse that sounded plausible, "I really miss them badly. I just got lost in a daydream. What's the matter?"

The familiar frozen orange landscape and barren lifeless plain had definitely returned. She did not know what she had seen only a few moments ago but she was determined to let nothing undermine her sanity. Ilya had rushed back to the pyramid and was excitedly pointing to a spot on its east wall. He was shouting for her to come and look. She was taken aback by the degree of his enthusiasm and felt that he must have discovered something really special. She quickly got to her feet and walked over to him.

On a section of the pyramid which was particularly heavily encrusted with red dust there seemed to be a series of slight bulges. As Ilya eagerly began to clear away the deeply ingrained dust, the object below came into clearer focus. Again Mary tried to dismiss it as her eyes playing tricks upon her. For the first time she was beginning to get worried about her sanity. 'Maybe there is something wrong with me?' she thought to herself. However, when she looked again the bulges were still noticeable. When she saw that Ilya obviously saw them as well she felt better. She kneeled down beside Ilya and helped him to brush away the thick dust. The more dust they removed the more excited they grew. The more the object below the dust became uncovered, the greater grew the sense of their elation. When the object came into full view it almost blew their minds. For there, embedded within the side of the pyramid, was a black metallic plate upon which was inscribed an unknown language written in bright blue characters.

They were looking at an inscription in an alien language. The black metal plaque was square and exactly four feet long on each side. The alphabetic script upon it consisted of symbols arranged in horizontal lines periodically separated by short vertical strokes. Some of the symbols, such as the triangles, circles and ankhs, were familiar, and others, such as the convoluted circles and squares or the dotted and multi-lined characters, were totally unknown. Mary scanned the image of the script into the computer processor and awaited a response. The answer came in the negative.

"The translator does not recognise the language," Mary said in frustration. "This planet is turning up more mysteries than answers. I'm beginning to get annoyed. This little passage may hold the key to understanding everything about the pyramids and we can't even read it. We're so close and yet so far away. God help us!"

"Discovering it is achievement enough," Ilya declared triumphantly. "Lee's remark about the similarity between these structures and their Earth counterparts is flashing through my mind. Look carefully at the script. Some of those characters are familiar. The ankh was a widely used symbol in ancient Egyptian times. That again begs the question, what is it doing here on a Martian pyramid?"

"The same can be said for the circles and triangles," Mary said as she scrutinised the script. "I think it points to the fact there is a universal thread of common knowledge which runs throughout the universe. These are mathematical symbols and to me it suggests that the universe operates upon a core of sacrosanct laws and principles that are the same everywhere. I mean all the elements that we have identified here on Mars can be found in the Periodic Table. It is only the different ways in which these principles are able to manifest and express themselves that accounts for the diversity of the universe."

"As far as I'm concerned discovering it is enough!" Ilya exclaimed happily. "I'll leave all the heavy theorising to the academics back home. Just wait till the others hear about our discovery. We'll record every minute detail about it so that we can tell the others later back at the camp-site. They will be thrilled."

Meanwhile Josh, Kevin and Natasha were thoroughly absorbed in studying the Face. They studied it and its environs meticulously. The most impressive thing about the sculpture was its size and sheer geometrical beauty. Although the ravages of time and the centuries of battering by the elements made the structure look worn and faded, a shadow of its former glory, it was still breathtakingly beautiful to behold. The many cracks upon its surface did not detract from its majesty. It possessed a serene power that seemed to imbue it with a consciousness that defied description.

"It really is a beautiful piece of art," Natasha exclaimed joyously. "It is the sphinx of Mars."

"Only it's ten times larger and its origins are unknown," Josh said carefully as he scanned the structure. "It is sculpted from one massive piece of rock which I surmise must have already been lying here."

They had been able to determine it was made out of a volcanic rock similar to granite. Its age was judged to be a million years. However, the surrounding environment yielded no answers as to who might have built it. There remained not a single trace of the civilisation that had erected this monument, not a single artefact or implement. It was as if this structure was created elsewhere and then unceremoniously dumped in the barren landscape of Mars. Yet all knew this could not be true. Something had happened to the source civilisation that had built these monuments. The landscape surrounding it was the same barren cratered wasteland that constituted the surface of Mars and which made the presence of the Face and the other features that much more enigmatic.

"There are absolutely no indications as to who built it or what function it may have served," said Josh. "Maybe it was built for purely ornamental value or it could have been a symbol of some spiritual significance. Or it could be the portrait of an important personage from that time."

"I think it is the portrait of a former king or ruler," Kevin added thoughtfully. "What I find the most fascinating is the sheer size of the rock it was carved out of. It's absolutely colossal. The whole process must have taken years to complete."

"We don't know that for sure yet," Natasha interjected. "We have no idea of what kind of technology was used in its construction."

"For the time being, let's be satisfied with having been able to verify that it is indeed an alien artefact," Josh said. "We can leave the academic studies to the scholars on Earth. Our task is to compile and record as much data as we possibly can and take it back to Earth. As far as this structure is concerned there appears to be nothing more we can glean from it at present. Let's move on to the skyscrapers."

Natasha suddenly stopped still and shut her eyes. She stood like that for several moments and uttered not a single word. Josh and Kevin looked on anxiously but dared not disturb her. Natasha was chosen for her psychic sensitivity. The Russian Academy for Psychic Research had selected her as a small child because she showed unusual potential, and she had been put through an intensive training program before she moved on to become an astronaut. The two men, being fully aware of this, knew not to disturb her when she fell into one of these trance-like states. They had noticed that she had done this several times while they were travelling to Mars and she had often come up with startling insights in response to difficult questions. After several moments she opened her eyes and shook her head slowly from side to side as if she had just received shocking news.

"What's the matter, Natasha? Are you all right," asked Josh reassuringly.

"A figure appeared in my inner vision and his face was exactly the same as this stone face," she said. Her face had a look of bewildered excitement upon it. "If what I sense is true than it is truly fantastic! I believe I've just made telepathic contact with the Martian entity that is depicted by the Face. The fact that I've made contact means that he must still be alive; he must still be living on Mars and is aware of our presence!"

"Then how come our sensors haven't detected him yet?" Kevin asked.

"Our sensors are only capable of detecting organic life," Natasha replied slowly. "This entity no longer resides in a physical body."

"You mean it's a ghost!" Kevin exclaimed.

"In a manner of speaking," she replied. "This being exists on a vibrational level which is much higher than the frequency upon which our physical bodies and sense driven minds operate. I only managed to make contact by accessing the telepathic frequency within my mind. Although we cannot see it I feel certain it is aware of us."

"What does this experience mean?" asked Josh.

"I'm not sure," replied Natasha. "I think he was trying to tell me something. He was dressed in a long flowing robe and held what appeared to be a long staff with a glowing head. He was shaking his head and waving his left arm. I felt as if he was trying to tell us to leave this place. I think it might have been a warning for us not to stay here."

"Can you not re-establish the telepathic link and find out more?" Kevin asked.

"Telepathy is a two way thing," Natasha replied. "All the parties engaged in it must mutually agree. I cannot force it upon another being and I think this entity does not want to say anything further at the moment."

"Whether it was a warning or not, we're staying put until we've done everything we came here for. We didn't travel forty-eight million miles across space just to turn back at the first sign of trouble," replied Josh. "You're saying his face was identical to this statue?"

"Yes. This monument is made in his image," replied Natasha. "Who he is, I don't know. I sense he was a person of great importance. Maybe he was a king or an emperor or perhaps even some kind of divinity. Can't say for sure at the moment. The fact that I have been able to establish some kind of telepathic contact with him means that he must still be on Mars. We are definitely not alone."

"Could it be the same person that Mary claims she saw the other night?" asked Kevin.

"It wouldn't surprise me," she responded thoughtfully.

"This expedition is getting more interesting each passing moment," said Josh. "First we discovered these alien monuments. If that wasn't enough we had Mary's experience last night and now Natasha tells us there is some kind of Martian entity here watching us. What next? I wonder if the others have found anything. It's approaching twilight and we'll call it a day for today. We'll leave the skyscrapers for Dmitri and Lee tomorrow. Besides, they don't look that appealing anyway. Let's get back to the camp and hear what the others have to say."

They glanced over their shoulders to look at the skyscrapers as they made their way back to the camp. It had to be admitted there was something about them which was disturbing, even sinister. The other monuments all elicited a sense of wondering excitement. These structures did that as well but there was something else about them which caused irrational feelings of fear and trepidation to arise. Perhaps it was simply their grim appearance. Their ugly dark brown colouring and impenetrable fortress-like appearance did not help to endear them to the astronauts' hearts in the same way as the Face and the pyramids had done.

Natasha stopped for a while as she trailed the two men. She turned around to look at the skyscrapers once more. As she did so a shudder went down her spine and an icy cold chill came over her surpassing the chill of the environment in which she stood. For a split second she thought she heard a noise from within the towers. It lasted only a fraction of a second and could so very easily have been nothing but a figment of her imagination. Yet she distinctly remembered the sound she had heard. It sounded like the angry rabid howling of a dangerous beast that wanted to be released. Natasha touched her forehead and crossed her heart uttering a small prayer of protection and turned to join her friends.

7

Josh and Natasha returned to camp to find Lee and Dmitri working on the magnetic electrospectrometer. They had been analysing soil and rock samples picked up from the vicinity. They greeted the newcomers enthusiastically and offered them some coffee. Dmitri said that the soil was heavily laden with iron oxide as were the rocks. But that was something already known by Earth scientists and elicited no great interest from anyone.

"We've only just got up," Dmitri said. "Considering the time of day we thought we'd leave our explorations until tomorrow."

"How was it?" asked Lee inquisitively. "Did you find anything interesting?"

"We have been able to amass a great deal of information about the physical structure of the Face but are not any closer to discovering the identity of its builders," Josh answered thoughtfully. "However, Natasha did have an interesting experience. But we'll wait until the others get back before we discuss it."

"What happened?" Dmitri spoke directly to Natasha, reverting to his native Russian in the process.

"I had a psychic experience. I made contact with the Martian entity whose face is depicted by the stone Face," responded Natasha, likewise in Russian.

"Natasha, you know I don't believe in this psychic stuff, and I think deep down you know it's not true. Then why do you carry on putting so much store by these things? What you experienced was simply a mental aberration brought on by stress. What's the point of blowing it up into some kind of weird explanation which has no basis in scientific fact."

"Well excuse me," exclaimed Natasha. "You're entitled to your opinion but I don't think you're in any position to judge. My abilities have been well documented and tested and I don't have to justify myself to you or anybody else. I know beyond any possible doubt that there is a Martian entity present on Mars. Mary has already encountered it and I have been able to establish some kind of telepathic contact which may well prove fruitful at some future time."

"Suit yourself," Dmitri said as he pushed the matter aside with a shrug of his shoulders.

"Speak English please," Josh called out. "We're all in this together and must hide nothing from each other."

Dmitri apologised and reassured Josh that nothing covert had been said. Within thirty minutes the other teams, apart from Mary and Ilya, had arrived back. Everyone milled around the coffee urn. In this cold environment drinking piping hot cups of coffee felt like sheer luxury. They all admired the stunning sunset. Its bright pink hue stood in dramatic contrast to the deep star-decked purple canopy that stretched out above them. The twilight hours on this planet afforded the most beautiful views of glorious sunsets which no place on Earth could ever hope to match.

When Mary and Ilya did arrive they rushed, rather than walked, in. It was clear they were excited about something. Mary blurted out that they had found an inscription on the side of their pyramid. This drew gasps of astonishment from the rest. Ilya passed around photographs of the script. He explained that they had spent many hours studying it but were unable to translate it. The discovery of an alien script caused much heated controversy. There was a strong desire to go and look at the script immediately. However, darkness was rapidly descending and Josh felt it was better left until later as the mission had to run to a strict schedule.

Each of them offered an opinion on what the text might mean. Lee felt it was some kind of warning against entering the pyramid, reminding the others of the fate of the people who broke into the tomb of Tutankhamen after disregarding a similar warning. Ilya felt it might contain a secret code for gaining access to the interior of the pyramids. Lorna preferred to believe it was simply an ornamental plaque commemorating the builders of the structure. After several minutes of argument it was decided to let the matter rest for a while since nobody really knew the truth. The pictures of the writing would be transmitted back to earth and the scientists there could begin working on it.

The two teams studying the pyramids concurred on the remarkable uniformity of their construction and the type of building material used. The technology used to effect their remarkable design must have been very advanced. This was especially evident from the fact that a single piece of material had been moulded into a pyramid. This contrasted dramatically with the earth pyramids where countless blocks of stone had to be painstakingly put together. For the Martians to have done what they did represented a huge technological gap in their favour. Although the specific purpose for their erection could not be accurately pinpointed a couple of possibilities were suggested. Firstly they might have served a symbolic purpose of a religious or mystical nature. Lorna also suggested that as they were aligned to the magnetic north pole of the planet and, in addition, in direct alignment to the Pleiades star system, they could quite conceivably have served as a kind of planetary beacon for spacecraft. The others weren't quite sure whether Lorna was serious when she said this but the suggestion brought forth a light-hearted riposte from Dmitri who thought she was letting her imagination get the better of her.

"Dmitri, don't be so quick to dismiss things you don't understand!" Mary cried out in mild annoyance. "Did you expect to find these monuments on Mars?"

"No, I didn't," Dmitri replied casually.

"I would rule nothing out," Mary continued. "Standing here on this planet and looking up at that huge universe up there I now, more than ever, am overwhelmed by the glory and wonder of the cosmos. To think that for the last few days we have been living amongst monuments constructed by an alien race that was technologically advanced whilst we on Earth were still living in caves and wearing animal pelts has humbled me completely. I mean just think of it, at one time intelligent beings lived here. I wonder what they looked like? What they were called? What kind of lives they lived? Why they built these things? What happened to them? These and a million other questions are passing through my mind. I would dearly love to find out the answers. Perhaps these pyramids were beacons for spacecraft or maybe they served an even more fantastic purpose? I am prepared to believe anything."

Behind Mary's outwardly calm appearance lay a tumultuous mind. Lorna's comment had started her thinking. In her dreams she recalled seeing flying vessels that were probably spacecraft. To her way of thinking, if those dreams she had were a glimpse of past times on Mars then these pyramids might have served a purpose similar to what Lorna had postulated. Mary did not feel comfortable enough at the moment to discuss her dreams, fearing it might only make the others laugh at her, especially her cynical Russian male colleagues, whose presumptuous arrogance she often found mildly irritating. Yet she knew they were basically good decent men and deep down she was fond of them. She especially did not want to tell the others of the vision she had had at the pyramid when that vast plain turned into a sea for a few minutes. That would really convince them she was going crazy.

Josh listened carefully to the reports his team gave of their day's work, his sharp analytical mind taking in every minute detail. The discovery of the metallic plates with the alien inscriptions was in itself a momentous event rivalling the discovery of the monuments themselves. They now had in their possession a piece of writing that originated from an alien mind which would, when translated, yield invaluable insights into the psychology of an alien race. Josh told the others about their work with the Face and then told them Natasha had something to say.

"While we were studying the face I received a strong telepathic impression," she started. This did not surprise the others for by now psychic research and development, although still viewed sceptically in many quarters, were taken seriously by all major governments. Every school child on earth now had a lesson each week on the development of psychic potential, with the ones who showed exceptional promise being streamed off into special classes.

"I made contact with a Martian entity," she continued. "I feel certain it is the same person whose face is depicted by the monument. Whoever, or whatever it is, is still on Mars. I did not feel it to be a hostile presence. However, I feel certain it was trying to warn us against something. The telepathic contact did not last long enough for me to establish any more details."

"What did it look like? Does it have a name?" asked Mary excitedly.

"I don't know its name. All I can say is that it was a very tall male with long cascading hair," replied Natasha.

"That's exactly what I saw!" exclaimed Mary loudly. "You see! I didn't have a hallucination. Natasha has just confirmed that there is something in my experience. There is life on Mars. Maybe not in the way we understand it, but it exists. I know it."

"Now I really am spooked!" Lee shouted. "You mean to say there really is some kind of Martian out there. It could be watching us right this very moment. Who knows what it might have planned for us? I would love to get my hands on that damned fool who advised that weapons were not necessary for this mission! While he's sitting safely at home we are now facing an unknown peril here on this god-forsaken planet. I would feel a lot better if we had brought some of those newly-designed electron pistols. I sure hope this Martian is friendly otherwise we might be in real trouble."

"All right, that's enough, Lee," Josh interjected with mild irritation. "Control yourself. There's nothing we can do about that now, and it's stupid to allow irrational fear to get the better of you, especially since we haven't really encountered anything dangerous or life-threatening yet. Natasha said that she didn't think this entity was hostile and that's good enough for me. Judging from Mary's experience I think this Martian is content to simply observe us. Besides, we're only here for a few more days, so let's keep our energies focused upon finishing our mission successfully. With any luck we may be able to finish it and return home without any further dramatic incidents. There is absolutely no point in getting distracted by unnecessary fear, imaginary or otherwise."

"If there's one of them there could be more. Who's to say the others aren't hostile," exclaimed Lee. "Natasha herself said that it was trying to warn her against something. Maybe whoever she contacted is not dangerous, but what about the thing this person was trying to warn her about?"

"That will be all for today," Josh said firmly. "Tomorrow Lee and Dmitri can start work on the skyscrapers. The rest of us will go to the source of the pulsating energy we detected whilst onboard the Ares. It is located thirty kilometres from here in close proximity to a large mountain range and seems to be surrounded by a mass of large objects, possibly huge rocks or maybe even more structures such as the ones we have encountered here. We won't know for sure until we get there. We will take the transporter and depart at dawn. It is best we stay overnight once we get there. Now let's get some sleep."

They prepared to retire for the night. It was slightly colder than the previous night with the temperature standing at minus ninety-eight degrees. The astronauts had often thought to themselves how miraculous it truly was to be able to exist and operate in such an extremely cold environment which also lacked the right kind of atmosphere for them to survive in under normal circumstances. The Martian Conditioning Process was a fantastic breakthrough and they were all very impressed by how well it was working. Although they were nervous at first because they were, in a way, guinea pigs to test the effectiveness of the process, the fact that it had worked so exceedingly well was both a relief and a source of great delight. It also meant the process could be modified to suit different planetary conditions on future missions to other planets. They were in more than one way acting as true pioneers of space travel. Their experiences here would be assiduously studied by Space Academy and the knowledge gained would help plan future space missions, and this was all on top of the totally unexpected breathtaking discovery they had made of an extra terrestrial civilisation. This trip would go down as the most successful in the history of space exploration so far and they were all immensely proud to be part of it.

Lee and Dmitri were not quite ready for sleep and decided to take a small walk around the periphery of their camp-site as they drank their coffee.

"Trust us to get assigned to those damned skyscrapers!" Lee said angrily. "I wanted to study those pyramids. It could have been us who discovered that metallic plate. Now those two will bathe in glory when we get back to Earth."

"It doesn't matter Lee!" Dmitri exclaimed. "We're all in this together. We shall all share equally in the glory of whatever discovery anybody makes here. There is no place here for petty jealousy and rivalry. We simply can't afford them here. We have to stick together and work as one closely knit team. This is not Earth, this is Mars! Don't ever forget that. Any breakdown in harmony amongst us here will cost us dearly. We simply can't survive without each other. I mean we can't just pick up a phone and call the ambulance or police if something goes wrong with one of us. We have no choice but to depend on each other. Here on Mars we are all links in one chain. If even one link turns defective it could have catastrophic consequences for all of us. Besides, who's to say we won't make the most sensational discovery of the entire mission tomorrow at those much maligned skyscraper structures. Nobody really likes them very much but they might be holding the most significant secret of the whole planet."

"Yeah, I know you're right," Lee answered. "I wish Natasha had kept her mouth shut about this alleged Martian that's supposed to be hovering around here. She's only succeeded in making me feel more nervous than I already was. Now when I'm working I'll be constantly on edge."

"There's nothing to worry about. Let's just finish our work and go home," Dmitri replied. "I am looking forward to returning home and spending three months with my wife and children in our dacha by the Black Sea. It will be especially lovely in the summer."

"Yes I'm sure it will," Lee responded happily. "Especially after a week here. I for one will see Earth in a new light. Never again will I ever take anything for granted. The first thing I'm going to do when I get back home is make hot passionate love with my wife non-stop for three months."

"Sounds wonderful. I'll think I'll do the same as well," the Russian responded with a broad smile.

The two men walked over to the tent and joined their comrades for another night's sleep.

8

Lee and Dmitri were the first to awaken the following morning and they wasted no time in getting ready to depart. Lee in particular wanted to absorb himself in studying the skyscrapers in an attempt to keep his fears at bay. He had come to Mars genuinely believing it to be an uninhabited planet. Although the discovery of the monuments had been a surprise they only proved that a civilisation had once existed. The fact that no organic life had been detected had served to reassure him that the planet was totally lifeless. In his wildest dreams he had not expected to be confronted with the possibility of facing life-forms of a more ethereal nature. Nevertheless, he tried his best to reassure himself by telling himself that all this talk about Martian entities was nothing but hysterical nonsense from over-emotional women and that Josh was foolish in giving it even the slightest credence.

"You know something, Dmitri, I'm scared," Lee said suddenly.

"I'm surprised to hear that, Lee," Dmitri replied. "You always struck me as being a very confident man. What makes you say something like that?"

"Being here spooks me," Lee said slowly and carefully as if he was weighing every single word. "I can't wait to leave this place and get back home. I promise myself never to volunteer for another space mission again. This aura of confidence is something I manufactured. It has worked so well that not only have I fooled everyone around me I have also fooled myself. But now that I'm here on this planet I have nowhere to run to. Inside I'm trembling with fear and my nerves are frazzled. These past few years I managed to convince myself I wanted to come to Mars. I convinced myself so well I passed all the tests and have finally got here. But now that I'm here I hate the place. I've never seen such a god-forsaken hell-hole in my life. I've got a really bad feeling about today. Don't know why but I can't shake it off."

"But why did you volunteer?" Dmitri asked. "You didn't have to and I know your family were totally opposed to the idea. So why did you do it?"

"I just wanted to prove to myself and others that I could accomplish something truly outstanding," Lee carried on. "Well, I've certainly done that. Being a member of the first manned expedition to Mars is certainly a noteworthy achievement. But I did it for all the wrong reasons. I did it purely for selfish and egotistical reasons. I had a point to prove and I proved it. Unlike you and all the others, I'm not here because I love adventure and exploring the unknown. Now that knowledge is staring me straight in the face and I don't know how to deal with it."

"The best way to deal with it is to focus on the job in hand," Dmitri replied reassuringly. "You're an invaluable member of the team and I certainly need your help today in studying those skyscrapers. Push your fears and self doubts away. We don't need them, neither can we afford them. We've only got a few more days left. You've made it this far and I'm sure you'll make it through to the end. Trust me."

These words from the Russian appeared to calm Lee down, and he resolved to concentrate upon the task in hand. He poured himself another cup of coffee and ate some eggs and fruit. The others quickly emerged soon after the two men. They greeted each other jovially and tucked into the breakfast that they had prepared. There was not much time for chat this morning. Josh directed everyone to prepare for the trip to the energy source. The transporter was loaded up with all necessary supplies and equipment and everyone except Lee and Dmitri got into the vehicle. There was a sense of excitement in the air at the prospect of travelling to a new site and possibly making new discoveries. Already the monuments they had discovered here were beginning to take on the tarnished edge of familiarity. Just before the vehicle was due to depart Josh walked over to the two men who were to remain behind.

"We're ready to leave now," Josh started. "I'll leave this camp in your capable hands. Those structures will keep you occupied for a long time. They look rather forbidding don't they? The place where we are headed is comfortably within communicator range. Contact us immediately if there is any problem."

"We'll be fine, Josh!" Dmitri said confidently. "I'm really looking forward to studying those structures. You never know what they might reveal. I'll compile a full report."

"Lee, how are you feeling this morning?" Josh asked.

"I'm fine, Josh," he replied. "Sorry about last night. I was a bit out of order."

"Think nothing of it," Josh replied. "There's nothing wrong with having a vivid imagination, even if it does carry you away sometimes. I'm sure we'll discover this mysterious energy source to be nothing but some kind of natural phenomenon. Just a few more days and then we can start heading back home."

"Amen to that," Lee exclaimed.

Josh walked back to the transporter and climbed aboard. The vehicle powered up with the familiar low drone and moved forward. The others inside waved the two men goodbye. As Lee waved back a disturbing thought flashed through his mind. It only lasted a fraction of a second but it shook him to the core of his being. Worse still, he could not account for it in any rational way. As he waved at his friends in the vehicle the thought passed through his mind that this would be the last time he would ever see them. Almost instantaneously he dismissed this thought as being the morbid out-cropping of a stressed body and mind. He forced his attention back to the task at hand.

The two men hastily gulped down their coffee and jumped to their feet. They retrieved their bags from the other transporter and walked the short distance to the skyscrapers. It took just ten minutes for them to reach their destination. They surveyed the morose looking structures and were impressed by the sheer strength they exuded. They stood in proud defiance of the cold indifferent world which so begrudgingly housed them, as if to proclaim their indomitable spirit of endurance.

They commenced their study eagerly. In all, there were six structures varying in height from one hundred to two thousand feet. They were brownish black in colour and all were made out of a material that resembled marble in texture and appearance. Their scanning devices were unable to penetrate the outer walls of the structures. They found this puzzling because the walls were nowhere near as thick as those of the pyramids and therefore should have been much easier to scan through. Lee scraped off a tiny portion of the outside wall of one of the structures and examined it under an electron microscope. Dmitri carried on walking around the structure assiduously studying every small detail. Suddenly he became aware of something.

"Have you noticed anything unusual?" he called out.

"In what way?" Lee shouted without taking his eyes away from the microscope.

"The temperature," Dmitri responded.

Lee looked up from the microscope and looked around. When he gave the matter serious attention he realised that it was in fact warmer here. At first he tried to dismiss it as nothing but an ordinary fluctuation in temperature but the degree of warmth was startling. He told Dmitri to get the thermometer from the vehicle and take a temperature reading. While the Russian was doing this Lee went back to the analysis of his wall sample. A shout from Dmitri distracted him again.

"When I passed that large boulder I noticed a definite fall in the temperature," he shouted. "I've got the thermometer. The reading here is minus fifty-four degrees Fahrenheit. I shall start walking towards you now. I am now approaching the area where I experienced the fluctuation... what the...!"

"What's the matter?" Lee shouted back as he saw his friend suddenly stop in mid stride.

"The temperature has just risen by thirty degrees," Dmitri exclaimed excitedly. "The heat must be coming from those skyscrapers."

Lee got up and walked to his friend and looked at the thermometer. Astonishment gripped both men as they realised there must be an internal energy source within these structures which was still active. Yet their instruments had picked up no sign of any unusual activity. They walked towards the largest building and as they neared it the temperature rose. When they stood next to it the temperature stood at one degree above zero, which by Martian standards was positively tropical.

"No wonder I felt so warm here," Lee exclaimed. "It just didn't register because I was so preoccupied with my own thoughts. It's got to be coming from within these towers."

"The heat only extends to a distance of twenty feet around the site," said Dmitri. "That's why we haven't detected it yet. All this time the others were more interested in the Face and the pyramids, not realising that these unattractive-looking things might have yielded more significant discoveries. Now it's our turn. You see! What did I tell you last night? These structures might be holding the most important discovery on the whole planet. Be grateful that it's we who have been given the chance to uncover it. Fortune really does seem to be smiling on us."

The two looked at the towers with renewed fascination. They racked their brains in an attempt to discover a way to get inside the structures but they could see nothing that might serve as a doorway to the interior. Unlike the skyscrapers on Earth, these ones had no openings into which at one time doors or windows might have been inserted.

"How were the people who used to live inside these things able to look outside. There's no place for any windows or doors," Lee spoke out as he studied the readings on his scanning device. "They are hollow inside but I can't work out what's inside them. Something is blocking the scanning ray. They're constructed out of a form of granite which is exceedingly hard. Their construction is more akin to a fortress than an office block. However, I can't see any entrances. Can you?" said Lee.

"No, I can't either," replied Dmitri. "I think we are making the mistake of applying Earth logic to Mars and I don't think it works that way."

"What do you mean by that?" asked Lee.

"On Earth people live and work in skyscrapers," responded Dmitri. "It could be we are mistakenly thinking that these skyscrapers served the same purpose here. What if we're wrong? Maybe they served a different purpose all together. Just look at them. Do you see any windows? Do you see any doors? Yet our instruments tell us that they are hollow. Why are they hollow? It suggests to me that the builders did that deliberately in order to get inside them to perform a specific task. If all they wanted was a simple monument why not just erect a massive slab of rock and shape it into something like the Face."

"I have an idea!" exclaimed Lee. "I know strictly speaking it's not allowed, but I feel sometimes you have to bend the rules somewhat. I propose detonating a small explosive device so that we can put a hole in this building. In that way we can get to look inside."

Dmitri thought long and hard. It was clear he had serious misgivings about this suggestion. Yet it was also clear that part of him wanted to try it. He was just as anxious as Lee to look inside the enigmatic structure, especially now that they realised there was something inside which was emitting heat. This discovery could make all the others pale into insignificance. Of course, he knew that the mission regulations specifically prohibited unauthorised explosive detonations upon an alien planet, the reason being to minimise damage to alien environments and artefacts. A peculiar aspect of his Russian psyche was a strong tendency towards conforming to the requirements of authority. Undoubtedly, to embark upon the proposed course of action was risky and potentially dangerous. However, the compulsion to look inside the skyscraper was growing stronger each passing second. Finally his scientific curiosity got the better of him and he decided to be adventurous. He knew he would have to answer to Josh Walters afterwards but if, by gaining access to the interior of the building, they were able to make an astonishing discovery of some kind, then the anger of the rest of the team would be muted.

"All right!" Dmitri said with rising excitement. "Use only a small amount of explosive. Just enough to knock a hole in the side big enough for us to get in. I really would like to see what's inside these things."

"Yes, sir!" Lee replied enthusiastically. He rushed to the transporter and retrieved a small red box which contained the explosive material.

Walking back quickly, Lee opened the box and very slowly and carefully took out a small portion of the white liquid with a tube linked to a small electronic pump. The white substance was poured into a phial and a lid was then placed on the phial to stop the fumes escaping. Walking quickly over to the tower, Lee laid the explosive charge at the base of the eastern face. Both men stepped back to a distance of fifty meters. Lee pressed the button on the remote detonation device he held in his hand. The explosion was quiet but powerful. Once the dense white smoke had cleared, a gaping hole some seven feet in diameter and ten feet in height was revealed. Lee leapt into the air in excitement only to discover his lead-laden boots nearly caused a sprained ankle when he landed. Dmitri laughed.

The two men walked to the gap and tentatively put their heads inside. What they saw was no disappointment. The interior was cavernous and the walls were lined with transparent circular boxes which contained glowing purple globes. There were thousands of them arranged in neat orderly columns with a two foot gap between each box. In this one skyscraper there were at least thirty thousand.

They entered and looked around. The first thing that struck them was the heat inside then that the atmosphere was highly charged with a tangible electromagnetism.

The sight of the glowing globes mesmerised them for several moments.

"What the hell are they?" Lee shouted in feverish excitement.

"I've got no idea," replied Dmitri. "But they look fascinating. I guess they're some kind of energy forms."

"It's hot in here!" Lee exclaimed. "The heat's obviously coming from these globes. The whole place is reverberating with electromagnetic energy. It's so thick I can almost touch it with my hand... and the heat! It's like an oven in here! How come we weren't able to detect this incredible resonance from outside?"

"The external walls obviously blocked the energy from getting out," Dmitri said.

"I wonder what's inside these things?" Lee mused to himself as he looked closely at one of them.

"The outer container is a form of glass but it's incredibly strong," Lee said as he tried with all his strength to crack the transparent surface of the container. "I can't even put a crack in it."

"Don't do that! You might damage it," Dmitri shouted in horror as he watched his friend try to crack the container.

"Relax, will you. There are thousands of these containers in here. It's no big deal if one of them is damaged," Lee retorted angrily. "Besides, it appears to be a really tough cookie. It's not budging, no matter how much pressure I apply to it. It can't be glass otherwise it would have shattered by now. Hey, I have another idea. Why don't we try another explosion to open up one of these boxes?"

"No, it's too risky. We don't know enough about the kind of energy these boxes contain," Dmitri replied. "It could be dangerous and I don't want to push our luck. We are lucky our initial gamble has paid off. Josh may be annoyed with us but when he sees all this I'm sure he'll understand. I'm going to get on the communicator now and inform the others of our discovery. When they hear about this they'll drop everything and head right back here. Come on, let's go outside, it getting too warm for me in here."

They quickly walked outside. However, unknown to the two men, their explosion had changed something inside the structure. Something which had stood intact and sheltered for countless millennia had been traumatised by the rude jolt. The explosion had managed to crack the surface of some of the transparent containers. As a result the purple globes they contained suddenly came to life with a greatly increased level of intensity. The intensity of the glowing globes within the cracked containers became so great that in the end they shattered their containers and floated free within the tower.

The two men stood outside, engaged in conversation, oblivious to the chain reaction taking place inside the tower, which they had themselves unwittingly instigated. Dmitri was just about to activate his communicator when he was distracted by a noise coming from within the skyscraper they had just left. The sound was identical to that made by an electrical generator. It was loud and the vibrations of the sound caused the entire structure to shake. The two men looked around in startled alarm. Dmitri dropped the communicator to the ground. The sight of such a huge solid building trembling as if it might crash down upon them at any moment filled them with dread. Nevertheless, even though the sound was horrendous in its intensity and the vibrations it induced were terrible, the structure did not fall apart. It was possessed of enormous power and resilience, as if it was designed to withstand such vibrational battering.

"What the hell is that," Lee suddenly exclaimed. He pointed a finger at the gaping hole that had been his own idea.

From out of the hole emerged a floating ball of purple light. It was identical to the small globes that they had seen before but now it had grown enormously. This was shortly followed by another and then another. Very soon there were more than twenty of these glowing purple balls hovering above them. Each ball was now ten feet in diameter. No sound emanated from them but they seemed endowed with an innate intelligence that the men intuitively recognised. The invisible pulsing energy that emanated from the balls enveloped and permeated every cell in their being. They could sense what was happening but were powerless to resist. It felt as if they were being scanned by a scorchingly bright light which was studying every cell and fibre of their body and examining every section of their minds. Nothing was beyond the reach of the harsh invisible spotlight that scoured the very core of their being.

"What the hell are they and what are they doing to us?" said Lee in a quiet tone. Inside he was raging with anger and indignation at being so psychically violated but he could not express it verbally. All he could manage was the faint tone that dropped from his mouth.

When he tried to move his arms and legs he found they were paralysed. It was as if he was frozen to the spot on which he stood.

"Don't move," said Dmitri in the same anguished, subdued tone of voice.

"Are you kidding?" replied Lee. "If I could move I wouldn't be standing here, that's for sure."

"They must be the energy sources we detected within the boxes," Dmitri continued slowly and agonisingly. "Our explosion must have released some of them. They are scanning us. I feel an invisible wave of energy probing my mind and body. Do you feel it too?"

"Yes I do," replied Lee. "I wonder what they are? I hope they are friendly. It was a mistake to blow a hole in that building. I'm so sorry I put the idea in your head. What if the Martians built those skyscrapers to keep those things inside?"

"Maybe, but it's too late now," replied Dmitri.

The purple globes that hovered above them contained menace of a kind so great that words could never express it. The two men could sense deep hatred and anger being directed at them, the likes of which they had never ever encountered before. The sheer intensity of the negative, fear-inducing energy that was bombarding them was so overwhelming that it caused a paralysis of every system in their minds and bodies. As the two watched helplessly a recollection covering the entire span of their lives flashed through their minds in a split second. From time to time, for the span of a few seconds, the glowing globes would display within them a face, a definite individual face with a distinct personality. These seemed to represent the individual identity of each globe because the faces were different for each sphere. Only one thing united the different facial expressions that intermittently flashed through the glowing purple globes. That one thing was a countenance warped by hatred and deep resentment, fuelled by an almost timeless raging anger. To come face to face with such a savage alien fury was too much for the two humans to withstand. Their will to live was demolished.

Suddenly two of the globes shot forth a thin purple ray. The two beams of light struck each man in the chest. This caused them to fall to the ground. Their senses were stunned and they lay there in a daze. They were aware of everything around them but were unable to do anything. The two globes which had released the beams then quickly floated over to rest two feet above the bodies of the stricken men.

After some moments the globes descended into the bodies and merged with them. The other globes then vanished into thin air.

9

The others were well on their way to the mysterious energy source. The caterpillar tracks of their vehicle proved admirably suited to the rough rock-strewn terrain they passed through. The smaller rocks were easily travelled over. When a rock was too big for the tracks to traverse the vehicle was steered around it. Along the way they saw many craters. At times they came across fissures in the ground that stretched for miles. Luckily for them none of these fissures blocked their way. It would have been extremely inconvenient if the Valles Marineris had blocked their way. It being 2400 miles long, it would have meant a detour of several days, and considering the time constraints of their mission, would have made locating this energy source totally impractical.

The most intriguing and exciting sights of all were the dried up river beds. Josh stopped the transporter at the edge of one of these channels. It was at least ten miles long and over seven hundred feet in depth. The parched fractured river-bed looked as if it had not held water in a million years. Rocks of varying sizes lay scattered all over it and there were many small craters inside. Natasha said that the craters must have been caused by asteroid collisions after the water had dried up. Otherwise the impact of the asteroids would have been absorbed by the water and these craters would not have formed. Mary remarked that, considering the size and number of these channels, Mars at one time must have been an incredibly fertile place. The rivers that existed then must have been enormous. From the vehicle, Natasha performed a scan of the river bed which again turned up no sign of any organic trace elements.

"We are approaching our destination," Josh called out. "It is now only two kilometres south east from here. We shall be there within half an hour."

"That must be the mountain range in which the energy source is located," Mary said as she pointed to the dark brown mass looming up in front of them. She did not mention the fact that for a split second she had seen deep lush vegetation extending up to the summit of the mountain range. Neither did she tell the others that amongst the orangy green vegetation she also saw scattered pagoda-like dwellings.

"They sure are," said Kevin. "I've never seen such a drab and lifeless range of mountains in my life. You know something: the more I see of this planet the more I realise how fortunate we are to live on our beautiful Earth. I really wish the people back home would appreciate our world a lot more. I'm sure if everyone on Earth spent a couple of days here their attitudes would change dramatically. When I look at that mountain range and compare it to the beautiful forest-clad snow-capped Rockies and Himalayas my heart feels saddened."

"Maybe they weren't like this all the time," Mary said quietly and thoughtfully. "What if at one time they too were like our own mountain ranges. What if at some point in the past this whole planet was a teeming lush paradise with oceans, rivers and huge expanses of forest teeming with strange exotic wildlife. The fact that these dried up river-beds exist proves that at one time there were rivers here. The fact that at one time there were large bodies of water on Mars means that the atmosphere must have been thicker and able to support life-forms." Again she did not mention that she had already had a brief glimpse of Mars in its state of former glory.

"Yeah maybe. I guess we'll never know," Kevin replied with a shrug of the shoulders. "They've certainly done a good job in hiding their remains, that's for sure. We have not been able to find a single bone or fossil. Yet those monuments prove that an advanced race of aliens once lived here."

"I have another idea," Yuri exclaimed. "It could be these monuments are not the creations of a former indigenous Martian civilisation. Maybe they were placed here from somewhere else."

"What exactly do you mean?" Lorna asked in a puzzled manner.

"Well it was you who suggested that the pyramids may be beacons for spacecraft," Yuri replied. "I think these structures may have been erected by a race of aliens from another world who simply used Mars as a staging post in their space travels. They probably erected similar monuments on other planets as well. Maybe they used this planet as a base for refuelling or mining precious minerals. Or it could have been a kind of interplanetary service station? Who knows? It's only an idea."

"Hah, you're sounding more like our American friends each passing day!" Ilya retorted in a half joking manner. "Yuri, I never realised you possessed such an extraordinarily vivid imagination. You should have been a novelist!"

"It certainly does provide food for thought," Lorna said.

Nobody really knew what to expect. The generally held consensus was that it was likely to be only underground thermal activity or a deposit of naturally occurring radioactive material. Most of them expected to see only more rocks or, if they were really lucky, more of those monuments they had already encountered. If they existed on one part of Mars there was no reason to suppose they could not be found elsewhere on the planet.

Soon the area they were looking for loomed up in front of them. It lay nestled at the base of the mountain range and from a distance it looked as if it was covered by several large rocks and hills. But as they got closer their excitement began to reach a level not yet reached so far. As the sight in front of them gradually came into clearer focus their sense of bewilderment grew exponentially. Was what they saw real? Was what they thought they were seeing a mirage or an optical illusion? If the sight in front of them was real then it truly surpassed everything they had experienced before. When they arrived they found their eyes were not mistaken. What they found were not more rocks and boulders. It was not even more of those wonderfully enigmatic structures they had discovered earlier. For there, right in front of their eyes, nestled at the foot of a dark forbidding mountain range, were the ruins of a Martian city.

"Am I really seeing what I'm seeing?" exclaimed Lorna Kelly in bewilderment. "Or is that really a Martian city?"

"It's real all right!" exclaimed Kevin.

The team leapt out of the transporter and ran towards the sight in front of them. They saw a city that looked very out of place in its surroundings. It was a sprawling expanse of predominantly white and orange structures. Although a centuries old layer of red dust encrusted the buildings, they still retained their majesty and silent dignity. The buildings were widely spaced with large expanses of barren ground between them. Throughout the city there meandered a worn black road which was made out of a metallic substance. When it was scanned the metal was revealed to be a compound of iron and titanium. In addition to this metallic road there was also a network of paved stone roads which intersected the city at many points. The yellow stone out of which these roads was constructed was pale and worn and at one time it must have had an extremely high golden lustre. The buildings varied in size from oval structures about fifty feet in height to imposing skyscrapers over five hundred feet tall. There were more pyramids but these were not as big as the ones encountered earlier. Large pillared buildings were littered all over the place and at the back of the city stood what could only be described as crumbling mansions.

A shout from Ilya brought the others running to his side. He was looking down at a deep depression in the ground. It was a huge deep circular pit with a flat surface at the bottom. Around the sides of the pit were terraces carved out of the rock. The whole pit was at least half a mile in circumference. Behind the pit stretched out a massive plain littered with the tediously common rocks and boulders and craters. The orangeness of the terrain around them complemented the pinkness of the sky in a striking and stark manner.

"This is too much for words to express," Lorna exclaimed wildly. "Discovering those monuments was wonderful enough, but a city, a whole city on Mars, is simply awesome. What will the people on Earth say when they hear about this? Our mission is not long enough even to begin studying all this. This place will be able to yield incredible amounts of new knowledge and understanding about an alien culture."

"I understand how you feel Lorna," Josh said. "However, I have no choice except to comply with the restrictions imposed by Space HQ. We just don't have the ability or the resources to extend this mission. We will have to leave a detailed exploration of this city to a later mission. All we can do is make a start. Besides, this mission has already exceeded our wildest expectations. I'm sure a hero's welcome awaits us all back on Earth. Let's be content with that for the time being. You can always apply to HQ to be a member of any future expedition to Mars. With the experience you've gained here, I'm sure you'll have no problem being accepted. None of us would."

"I'm glad I came, but once is enough for me," said Ilya. "The life on Mars is long gone. It has made me appreciate my home much more and I would like to spend the rest of my days in a vibrant life-filled ambience. We take our lives on earth so much for granted and do not truly appreciate what a wonderful gift life truly is. That realisation is the greatest gift this mission has given me. I, for one, will be happy to return home."

"I'm sure we all agree with Ilya," Natasha replied. "Nevertheless, for the time being we are on Mars, so let's focus our attention on Mars. We've still got five more days here and in that time we can learn a tremendous amount. The more we learn now the better equipped the future missions will be."

"Precisely!" exclaimed Josh in wholehearted agreement. "I want Natasha, Ilya and Kevin to perform an initial survey of this place. Don't enter any of the buildings yet. I want a detailed map of the shape and structure of this place, the type of materials used in the construction of the buildings, and last but by no means least, determine the exact spot of that energy source we came here to study. In all the excitement of this discovery we've almost forgotten the original reason for us to come here in the first place."

Nobody had noticed that Mary had walked off from them. She was standing thirty meters away from the rest of the group with her gaze fixed upon the city that stretched out in front of her. Josh glanced over at her and called out to see if she was okay. She did not respond and kept on staring directly ahead as if she had not heard.

Mary Morgan felt deeply uncomfortable. A look of puzzled awe was firmly implanted on her face. It was as if she was in a daze and knew not what to do. The sight of this ruined city had stirred uncomfortable emotions within her: sensations which combined an uncomfortable familiarity with mind-boggling strangeness. It was as if she knew this place from somewhere but how could she have done? After all, this was her very first trip to Mars. Then it struck like a bolt out of the blue.

"What's the matter with Mary?" Kevin said as he looked over at her. "She appears glued to the spot as if she can't take her eyes off the place. Perhaps the shock of finding this place has affected her more deeply than the rest of us. She always was a bit highly strung."

"The dream! the dream!" she suddenly shouted. "It's from the dream!"

Her sudden outburst brought the others running to her.

"Are you all right Mary?" asked Josh.

"I'm fine," she replied. "I've seen this place before."

"How could you have?" asked Ilya.

"In my dream," Mary answered. "You remember the dream I had. Well, in that dream I dreamt of a city. It didn't click at first because the city I saw in my dream looked so very different but now I can see these are the ruins of the city I saw in my dream. Absolutely no doubt about it. This is the city I saw in my dream. I am absolutely positive I saw this city."

"You'd better tell us more about your dream," said Josh.

"I had three dreams and it is the third dream that relates to this place. I dreamt that I was in a city, a bustling metropolis inhabited by millions of people. Weird looking but beautiful people with purple skins and long red hair. The city was beautiful and prosperous. Those metallic pathways used to have cars gliding upon them. The yellow paved pathways were for pedestrians. In between the buildings, where now lies only barren earth, used to be orange grass. I saw it all in my dream. That dried up river bed over there was a mighty river upon which the Martians used to sail their boats. All around us there was lush fertile countryside with many weird plants and animals. Then something terrible happened. Out of the sky appeared a fearsome armada of flying saucers which proceeded to destroy everything in sight. They destroyed the entire planet before they withdrew back into space. It didn't register with me at first because their present ruined state made the buildings look so different from the place I saw in my dream. But now there is absolutely no doubt in my mind. This is the place I saw. At least what remains of it."

"Have you any explanations for this?" asked Lorna.

"I am certain the city I dreamt about was a Martian city. Obviously not from the present day. I believe I travelled back upon the time track and saw this city at a point in ancient Martian history. I witnessed an historical event which took place a long time ago. Once the whole surface of Mars was a verdant paradise teeming with cities and a rich civilisation. Then it was all destroyed by attackers from space. Who they are, or why they did what they did, I simply don't know."

"Mary has been able to access the Akashic Records," Natasha said.

"The what records?" asked Yuri in bewilderment.

"There is a psychic theory that states that the lives of every soul in existence are recorded in what are called the Akashic Records," Natasha began slowly and thoughtfully. "Every single detail of a soul's actions and deeds in any lifetime are meticulously recorded in these records. These records are stored in a higher dimension and access can only be gained by those with the necessary psychic sensitivity and mental temperament. Mary evidently has this."

"Are you talking about the theory of transmigration which the Hindus talk about, and if so, what's that got to do with Mary's experience?" Kevin asked with a puzzled expression.

"Partly," Natasha replied. "There are those who accept the existence of soul and reincarnation as being absolute fact. In addition these are considered by them to be universal laws. Which means they are equally applicable to Mars as well as they are to Earth, or any other place in the universe for that matter. The souls of the Martians who used to live here have long since moved on to other forms and worlds. Yet everything they did whilst they lived here has been recorded in these records and that is what Mary has been able to tune into."

"Fine. We don't have time for a philosophy discussion," Josh interrupted. "Let's stick to what's relevant to our present circumstances. Mary, can you tell us what kind of people these old Martians were?"

"Not that much except that they were beautiful and proud-looking and possessed a sophisticated civilisation. However, in my earlier two dreams I did see another race of Martians intermingling with the long-haired Martians. In my first dream they were living harmoniously with each other. In the second dream they seemed to be at war with each other. By the third dream this other race seemed to have completely disappeared. The dream did not last long enough for me to gather more information."

"Maybe the other race were in those flying saucers you saw?" quipped Kevin.

"You don't honestly believe all this nonsense, Josh!" Ilya cried out in exasperation.

"Ilya! You're infuriating!" Natasha cried out. "Why can't you just broaden your horizons of thought a little bit. Are you really so surprised that I decided against becoming romantically involved with you?"

"Maybe Natasha," Ilya answered, "it's just that I prefer to accept only those things that I can see and hear with my own eyes and ears. I grant you, I was surprised to find these ruins here but at least they are physical things. They can be seen and felt. Their existence can be scientifically proved. The same cannot be said for all this weird stuff you're talking about."

"Let's just keep an open mind for the time being," Josh replied forcibly. "Right now we have more pressing concerns. Mary, I suggest you carefully monitor your dreams from now on. It may be an unorthodox but nevertheless useful way of gaining knowledge. The entries may not make much sense now but perhaps one day they might prove illuminating. You three had better get on with that initial survey I've asked you to do. It's vital that is completed before we start our in-depth study tomorrow morning."

The discovery of the city was deemed to be the most important discovery to date. The decision was taken to focus all energy and resources on its study. Besides, most of them felt that they could not learn much more about the other structures than they already had with their present resources and equipment. The other features, though important in their own right, were not as exciting as the discovery of the ruins of a city. They felt that the city might provide them with the answers that the other features had not done so far. They all agreed that a new base camp should be constructed at this site to facilitate the work of exploration. Lee and Dmitri would dismantle the old camp and transport everything to this new site for the camp to be re-erected.

"Dmitri, come in please," Josh spoke into the communicator. For a while there was no response. Josh repeated what he had just said. Then the voice of Dmitri came over. His tone of voice was slightly more subdued than usual but not enough to give anyone any cause for concern.

"Yes. What is it?" Dmitri responded.

"You're not going to believe this," Josh said enthusiastically, "but we've just discovered the ruins of a city. Can you believe that, an actual Martian city? What do you say to that?"

No reply came for a moment. This caused Josh to ask if his communication had been received. Eventually Dmitri responded that he was excited to hear about the city. Yet his tone of voice carried not the slightest bit of excitement. His voice came across again as a dull monotone very unlike Dmitri's normal quick and melodious speech manner. Josh asked about Lee and Dmitri reassured him that he was fine as well.

"We will establish a new base camp here," Josh continued as he brushed the matter aside. "Please could you and Lee interrupt your work and return to our old camp? You are to dismantle the old camp and bring the gear over here and we can then re-erect the camp. You have our co-ordinates."

"Yes," replied Dmitri, "we will get onto it straight away."

"Dmitri! You could sound a little bit more excited," exclaimed Yuri as he talked into his communicator. "What's the matter with you? I thought you would have been absolutely delirious after receiving this news. Did you hear Josh correctly? We have discovered a Martian city! What do you say to that?"

"I heard correctly the first time," Dmitri replied in the same dull monotone. "We look forward to seeing it for ourselves. I must go now and start dismantling the camp. We shall be with you just before twilight."

"Are you sure you're all right my dear friend?" Yuri inquired anxiously. "Your voice sounds very different."

"I'm fine. Stop pestering me. I'm tired, that's all. We shall see you all shortly," came the reply from Dmitri.

Yuri was puzzled and troubled by this strange behaviour. It was so uncharacteristic of Dmitri to behave in such a manner. Yuri placed the communicator back in his breast pocket. For a few seconds he tried to figure out why Dmitri was acting the way he was. Then he simply shrugged his shoulders.

"Let me talk to Lee," Josh said.

"Hello Josh, this is Lee. Everything is fine," Lee answered. His voice too now had the same dull monotonous tone.

"What have your studies of the towers revealed?" Josh asked.

"Nothing at all. They're simply stone monoliths which served no special purpose at all. We have absolutely no idea why they were constructed. We shall formulate a few theories as to possible origin and function when we get the time. Bye for now."

"I guess the physical and mental stress of this mission is getting to them as well," Yuri said to Josh. "Funny, I always thought those two to be the strongest amongst us."

"Yes, I thought Dmitri's reaction was rather subdued," said Josh thoughtfully. "I had expected him to be ecstatic when I told him about our discovery. Lee too. Oh well, I guess they're just tired, that's all. There's no point in worrying about it. I'm sure everything's okay. Come on, we've got work to do."

10

In a couple of hours the three team members reported back with their findings. The source of the energy had been pinpointed as being located deep beneath the larger of the two pyramids. Their initial surveys had still not been able to define its true nature but it had been determined that it was encased within a metal structure of some kind. However, since the energy source was located almost a kilometre beneath the surface it was well nigh impossible to gain access to it with this mission's resources and time constraints. Lorna and Yuri were assigned to study the pyramid and learn as much as they possibly could about the nature of the energy. The consensus was that there was nothing dangerous within the city and it was okay to begin a more detailed study. The team lost no time in starting to explore the city.

The most prominent structures were two tall imposing pillared constructions with flat roofs. The pillars were remarkably well preserved and the roof had only a few small holes. Each pillar was made out of red sandstone and had a circumference of ten feet. The buildings were of a rectangular construction with ten pillars on the long side and five on the short sides. Inside, the stone floor was smooth and looked worn. Thick layers of rusty orange dust enveloped the whole place and walking on the floor of the structure felt like treading upon a thick carpet composed of dust.

When Mary and Ilya stepped inside and looked at the rear wall they made an astonishing discovery. The walls had mosaic-like illustrations upon them. Mary shouted wildly in excitement and the two ran forward to stand in front of the illustrated wall. It showed tall long-haired people engaged in various kinds of activities. There were depictions of Martians in chariots chasing dragon-like creatures. They had long sword-like weapons that appeared to be discharging bolts of electricity from the tips. Overhead there were scenes of flying vessels. One scene seemed to show a collection of tall ships sailing upon a tumultuous sea whilst overhead flew a flock of reptilian birds. Another scene depicted a metropolis with tall buildings and a throng of people walking along the broad pathways that ran through the city.

"My dream showed me several of the scenes depicted here," Mary said as she surveyed the mosaic with concentrated attention. "Those bird-like creatures flying up above and the ships I can recall clearly. The people drawn here are also like the ones I saw in my dream. I can also recall the broad yellow pavements depicted here. It's a weird feeling to have the contents of a dream confirmed by such an unexpected and thrilling discovery as this mosaic. The attention to detail is stunning. It's almost like looking at a photograph."

"Those creatures that are being hunted look like dragons or dinosaurs," Ilya said as he scrutinised the picture. "Perhaps there were dinosaurs on Mars as well at one time. What if the dinosaurs on earth all originated here? I'm beginning to think that there is a greater connection between our two worlds than I ever could have imagined. The only thing is how did they get from here to Earth? Let's go look at the other building. There might be more of these mosaics there as well."

The other pillared building was considerably larger and did not prove to be a disappointment. The mosaics there were larger and more colourful and vivid. The scene depicted was grisly. It showed the long-haired race of people engaged in a vicious battle with horrid-looking demons who had bald heads and possessed the most terrifying faces. Bodies were strewn all over the place, many with decapitated heads and severed limbs. All the combatants were armed with the same electricity discharging rods shown in the other mosaic. Overhead were more of the flying vessels but it was not clear whether they were participating in the fray or if they were simply observing the terrible battle taking place below them.

"Looks terrible!" Ilya said. "It must have been some battle. I wonder what those bald monstrosities are?"

"I remember!" shouted Mary. "Those bald creatures are the other race of Martians that I saw in my first two dreams. This scene is depicting one of the battles they fought. This is all the proof we need that what I dreamt was an actual historical recall from the ancient history of this planet. Call the others over for a look. They'll be stunned when they see these mosaics. They are the first things we've discovered that give us a real insight into the nature of the former inhabitants of this world. I feel so excited! Right in front of us is a piece of Martian history. It's fantastic! From this scene we can deduce they were a fierce warlike people. The ancient depiction of Mars being the god of war does not seem to be far from the truth. I wonder how the ancients were able to make such an accurate correlation between Mars and war?"

Ilya's shouts brought the others running. When they saw the mosaics they too were stunned and pored over every minute detail. Josh remarked that this was the first piece of lifestyle evidence they had come across. It proved that the ancient Martians were a warlike people, or at the very least had a warlike streak in their nature. Natasha felt that the scene depicted two different races of Martians. She felt that the long-haired ones were benevolent beings who were defending themselves against the more evil-minded bald ones. Mary added that the flying vessels were either the ones she saw attacking the Martians or they could have been craft indigenous to the civilisation that existed at that time.

"Mars being depicted as the god of war seems very apt judging by this," Kevin exclaimed thoughtfully. His attention was riveted upon the mosaic as he tried to absorb every single detail. "Come to think of it, they're not really that different from us humans, are they? We humans are not exactly renowned for our peaceful natures. The number of people that have died in wars on our planet since the beginning of recorded history is colossal. I don't think we're in any position to judge the Martians."

"I'm not judging anyone," Mary said. "I'm simply relishing this incredible discovery and learning as much about it as I possibly can. Perhaps all the aliens who inhabit all the planets in the universe are not too different from us in their basic natures. It could well be they have the same struggles as us to rise above their lower base selves, to rise above their anger, greed and pride. It's just that some are better at doing it than others, and that makes them appear more advanced or evolved than us. I believe we all have the same potential to rise to a higher level of existence if we can surmount our base nature. Obviously these Martians did not do that well enough otherwise they would not have had to engage in this war. I would like to believe that on some other planets things like war and selfish competition have been totally eradicated, thus freeing the creative energies of their people to pursue more uplifting goals. They would be the truly advanced planets of the universe."

"Mary! At times you come out with some of the most amazing insights!" Kevin exclaimed in bewilderment.

"We are becoming quite used to making these startling discoveries," Josh remarked excitedly. "You know the drill. Record everything and collect as much information and knowledge as you can. That is all we can do on this mission. Apart from the energy source below the pyramid, to which we have no way of gaining access, our explorations of the other sites have not revealed anything as dramatic as these mosaics. The buildings are fascinating in themselves, especially since we consider that they are the very first examples of alien architecture that any humans have encountered. Nevertheless they are only buildings and they are not much different from our own back home. Some of them, in particular the one we're standing in now, look very familiar. It's like a Martian version of the Parthenon. Lee and Dmitri will be here within an hour and then we can help them to get the camp up. In the meantime let's get back to our explorations. Good work, Mary and Ilya."

Josh and Kevin walked back to the metallic pathways they had been studying before being interrupted by Ilya's shouting. Their instruments were able to detect residual traces of electromagnetism. It was only a tiny fraction of its former strength but the fact that it was still there after all this time indicated that the original source must have been exceedingly powerful. Kevin recalled the dream that Mary talked about in which she described cars that flew along metallic roads. He now said he could well believe her since at one time powerful electromagnetic currents flowed through them. Josh added that the Martians must have been very technologically advanced to have had vehicles that operated upon electromagnetic energy.

"These pathways represent ley lines," Kevin declared excitedly. "If what Mary saw in her dream was true then those vehicles must have been propelled above these pathways by the force of the electromagnetism that emanated from them. I am certain the source of the energy derives from the molten core of the planet itself. The Martians were somehow able to establish a channel to the molten core and then use the energy thus derived to polarise these metallic pathways so that they could serve as transit ways for their electromagnetic vehicles. It's fantastic!"

"Yes, an ingenious and pollution-free system of travel," Josh said in an impressed manner. "If only we could duplicate the process on Earth."

There were more pyramids scattered around the city but these were on a much smaller scale than the ones encountered earlier. The most common buildings were the oval ones which varied from the size of a small cottage to that of a stately mansion. These had gaps in their walls which might have served as windows. They were impressed by the well-laid design of the city which combined spaciousness with grace. In its heyday it must have been an extremely pleasing sight.

Natasha was busy studying the river bed. The thought that at one time the parched cracked bed she stood upon had been a thriving coursing waterway fired her imagination and enthused her explorations. She looked intently into every tiny nook and cranny, desperately hoping to find some sign of organic life. It would be a dream come true to find the skeletal remains of an ancient Martian fish or other form of alien marine life. However, the river bed proved as barren and lifeless as the rest of the planet. Not a sign remained of any of the life that may once have lived here. It was beginning to look as if the only life left on Mars was of the ethereal variety which was proving to be rather elusive in nature. Natasha slumped down on to the ground in exasperation and mild frustration. She looked up at the light pink sky above her and then with a deep sigh cast her eyes over the empty orange rock-strewn landscape around her. Even she was now beginning to tire of this planet and longed to go home. The realisation came to her that it is the inhabitants of a planet that imbue it with vitality and life. Without people a planet was nothing except a dull lifeless shell. Even Earth itself without people would be nothing but an empty shell and lonely, albeit a very beautiful one when compared to Mars as it stood now.

"What happened to you, Mars?" she said to herself silently as she contemplated her environment. "Why has every last trace of organic life been shorn from you? I feel certain that at one time you were a thriving life-filled world. What happened?"

Natasha's reverie was interrupted by a shout from Kevin. He and Josh were studying a stretch of the yellow stone road which ran alongside the river bed. They had seen her sitting on the ground. Natasha got to her feet and walked over to them. She explained her growing feelings of frustration and an ever increasing sense of home sickness. Josh replied that he understood perfectly and admitted that he too desperately missed his wife and children and longed to get back home. Natasha went on to explain that the river bed showed no trace of any life that may have existed within it.

"It doesn't matter. Photograph everything. Document everything," Josh directed. "The more information we can collect now the more data the folks back home will have to work on. You never know, they might be able to pick up something that we have overlooked. Don't forget that the first sign of life on Mars came from a meteorite that languished unrecognised in a museum for many years before its incredible hidden secret was discovered. Who's to say we might not take back with us something that will prove to be equally, if not more, stupendous."

By now the memory banks of their computers had filled up with an enormous amount of data. This mission had proved outstandingly successful in gathering knowledge and data about Mars which would prove invaluable in planning later missions. The crew of the spaceship Ares would be immortalised as the first true pioneers of Martian exploration.

Lorna and Yuri reported that the pyramids in the city were of the same type as those in Cydonia, the only difference being their smaller size. A couple more of those metallic plates with that unintelligible script had been discovered. Lorna felt certain they held the key to understanding the pyramids but all further progress would be blocked until they could be translated. They stood beside the coffee urn and gulped down copious amounts of the liquid while they discussed the day's findings. Ilya was particularly excited about the mosaics and explained that Mary was in the process of wrapping up the day's work and would join them shortly.

"We've all had an excellent day," Josh said cheerfully. "What, with the discovery of the mosaics and the establishment of the fact that there is something very unusual beneath one of the pyramids, even though we don't have any chance of getting to it on this mission, it has been a very productive and exciting day. Add to that the fact that we have been able to determine that at one time powerful electromagnetic currents used to surge through those black metallic pathways, more than likely for the purpose of propelling vehicles along them, and it has been an extraordinarily successful day. I'm very proud of all that we've accomplished so far."

"Yes indeed!" Yuri exclaimed. "And we've still got three more days left to go. Who knows what else we may be able to discover? The two pyramids here are identical to the two in Cydonia in shape and construction. They differ only in size and the fact that one of them has an enigmatic energy source below it."

Meanwhile Mary, having completed the study of the mosaics, walked over to stand at the edge of the pit in the ground. She wished to contemplate her amazing discovery and clear her head before she joined her friends. As she looked into the pit her mind flicked into a state of intense concentration. The surrounding environment became blotted out and all she could see was the huge pit in front of her. Then the scene before her changed. The terraces on the side of the pit filled up with cheering people. They were the same purple-skinned people she had seen in her dream. At the bottom of the pit was a gruesome sight. A group of heavily armed men were fighting a huge monster. The monster looked like a carnivorous dinosaur with horns on its head and long lethal spikes on its tail. The creature was fearsome and stood at over a hundred feet in height.

The gladiators fought it with long sticks which shot out barbed bolts of electricity. These caused the creature great pain but did not seem to impair its fighting prowess. Although of great bulk the creature possessed amazing speed. It leapt around on its two long muscular legs with great agility. It waved its long thick tail with deadly accuracy, the spikes inflicting terrible injuries on the gladiators unable to escape its path. It had two long clawed arms and a huge gaping mouth bedecked with savage teeth. Those gladiators it did not manage to spike with its tail it tore apart with the claws on its arms and feet. Others were impaled by the horns on its head. From time to time it would snatch a gladiator into its jaws and then drop the mangled corpse back on the ground. All around the arena lay the bodies of countless slain and wounded Martians. The crowd bayed furiously with unquenchable bloodlust. When the numbers of gladiators fell below a certain point a couple of side doors would open and another contingent would rush out to join the fray. Mary felt herself being irresistibly drawn into this terrible scene. However, a voice behind her snatched her away from her trance-like state of heightened awareness.

Mary turned abruptly to see Natasha standing there. Mary explained what she had just seen and repeated that it must have been another scene from Martian history which she had tuned into. Natasha agreed with her and said that she had a special gift. Mary revealed to Natasha that these flashes of clairvoyance were becoming quite common and she wanted to know what she should do with this ability.

Natasha advised her to record the details. Mary explained that she had been initially very reluctant to disclose these visions in case her mental fitness for the mission came to be questioned but now she felt quite comfortable with sharing her experiences with the others. As they talked, Ilya, Josh and Kevin joined them.

"Is this a private conversation or can anyone join in?" Kevin joked.

"Mary's just had another one of her visions," Natasha explained. "She's just a bit concerned about whether she should share it with the rest of us. She doesn't want to be thought of as mentally unstable."

"There's no fear of that any more, Mary," Josh replied sympathetically. "The events and discoveries of the last few days have made us all realise the folly of ridiculing things we do not understand. The mosaics have confirmed some of the details from your dreams. You mentioned long-haired people and flying saucers long before we even discovered the mosaics. No one will ever doubt or mock you again. You have my word on that."

"Thanks, Josh. I appreciate your confidence in me," Mary responded warmly. "I can confirm that this pit is an ancient gladiatorial arena. I just saw a scene in which gladiators were fighting a kind of dinosaur. The terraces around the edges were filled with spectators. I feel the wildlife that the Martians had to contend with was a lot more fierce and terrible than we humans ever had to confront. It would be like if dinosaurs still populated the forest and jungles that surround our cities and urban sprawls on Earth. The Martians went on regular expeditions to hunt and capture these creatures. Some of them ended up here in gladiatorial contests which were designed to test the manhood of young Martians."

"I can well believe it. It certainly looks like a gladiatorial cockpit," said Josh as he shot a quick glance into the pit.

"This proves that my power to time travel can occur in both the sleeping and waking states," Mary continued. "When I was at the pyramid at the old site I saw the plain beside the pyramid as it was in the distant past. It was a large inland sea with several big rivers feeding into it. I saw it clearly just before Ilya discovered the Martian script. I have begun to keep a log of my experiences. It might come in handy one day."

"Yes, you do that, Mary. It's an excellent idea. I'm prepared to back you up all the way and so will the rest of us?" said Josh.

"I will at least desist from making sceptical remarks," Ilya added.

11

It was late afternoon and the sound of an approaching vehicle heralded the arrival of Lee and Dmitri. The others were glad they had returned to join them, and looked forward to hearing about their work with the skyscrapers. Everyone stopped what they were doing and headed towards the incoming vehicle. It came to a gradual halt beside the coffee urn. For a few moments the two occupants of the vehicle simply looked at the city that lay in front of them. Their team members waved to them and shouted greetings. The two men did not respond but simply carried on staring at the city. The others assumed they were simply shocked by what they were looking at, as they had been when they first saw it, and it would take them a few minutes to settle down and adjust to the shock.

When Lee and Dmitri got out of the transporter they did not even appear to notice their friends. Instead they walked forward some meters to get a closer look at the place without actually entering the outer limits of the city. They carried on staring at the city. In fact it was more than a stare. The way they looked at it was more akin to a hostile glare, as if the sight of this place invoked memories that had lain dormant for a long time: memories which now flooded back to the surface, causing anger and rage. They did not speak but turned to look each other in the eyes. A look passed between them which contained a deep stratum of hostility beneath quiet knowingness.

Josh walked up to them and greeted them.

"Welcome back, we're all delighted to see you again," said Josh. "Anything interesting to report from the skyscraper structures?"

With slow deliberation Dmitri turned his face to look Josh straight in the eyes. A cold shudder went down Josh's spine. The look in Dmitri's eyes terrified him. There was a cold and callous feel about them which Josh had never seen before. Dmitri's green eyes normally had a joyous twinkle in them which reflected his zest for life, but now that inner light had gone only to be replaced with an eerie emptiness. No words passed between them but the silence was electric. Josh dismissed the matter from his mind by telling himself that the strains and stresses of the mission were getting to Dmitri and that he was simply tired as well as excited at seeing this city.

"You've made good time, boys," exclaimed Lorna as she walked up to greet them. "If we work hard we could have this camp ready before nightfall. We've all had a long hard day and would love to get some sleep. Besides I understand there is a dust storm heading our way and it wouldn't be any fun being caught out in it, would it now?"

Both Lee and Dmitri turned to stare at Lorna and now it was her turn to feel the shudder down her spine. Their eyes looked dull and expressionless and yet they had a penetrating quality about them which unsettled Lorna. To Lorna it felt as if the two dear friends she used to know were no longer present, and someone or something else was looking at her through their eyes. She felt as if her inner self was being mercilessly examined by an invisible scorching spotlight. Lorna stepped back almost against her will and took hold of Josh's arm for reassurance. By now all the other team members had joined them and were puzzled by this strange behaviour from Lee and Dmitri.

"Are you guys okay?" Josh asked.

"Oh yes! we're fine," they both blurted out together as if they had suddenly burst back to life.

"I was just a bit distracted by seeing this old city again," said Lee.

"You've seen this city before, Lee?" asked Josh in surprise at Lee's strange remark.

"No, no of course not. Just a slip of the tongue," replied Lee hurriedly, shaking his head quickly from side to side as if he was trying to clear some mental cobwebs.

"We've both had a very tiring day. We're tired, that's all," Dmitri swiftly intervened. "I must apologise for our state of mental distraction. We didn't mean to ignore you people. It was just the combination of physical and mental fatigue allied with seeing this wonderful sight, it took us totally by surprise and it took us a while to adjust. It won't happen again. I promise you. All we need is a good night's sleep and tomorrow we'll be as good as new. As soon as we get the camp up we will go directly to sleep."

"As far as the towers are concerned we have nothing unusual to report," Dmitri continued. "They're simply stone structures with no obvious function that we can think of. I think they might be Martian versions of the megalithic stones found on Earth. Besides, this city that you've discovered here makes everything else we've found fade into relative insignificance."

Dmitri's words seemed to reassure the others and the anxious expressions quickly passed from their faces. They themselves could perfectly understand the strains a mission such as this could place on the human system.

At this point Dmitri made a rather unusual request which raised a couple of eyebrows. Dmitri said that it was essential that Lee and himself have a separate tent all to themselves. When asked the reason why, all he would say was they had a lot to discuss about their work with the skyscrapers and they had to have absolute privacy in order to compile their report. Lorna exclaimed that they had no secrets from each other on this mission and she couldn't understand why they wanted to be separate from the others. Surely, Lorna said in a state of mild irritation, they could share their findings with everyone. Nevertheless Dmitri was adamant and after a moment's thought Josh granted him his request.

The shadows of twilight were beginning to descend and Josh was more concerned with getting the camp up before nightfall. Already strong gusts of wind had begun to circulate in their vicinity and this added a sense of urgency to the matter. Everyone now got stuck into erecting the base camp. While they were working, Melicia called in from the Ares for a chat with Kevin. She said that she was getting rather lonely being by herself in a spacecraft orbiting in space while all her friends were on the surface. Kevin replied the mission would last only another three days and then she would have them all back with her and it would be like one happy family again. This cheered her up and she told Kevin that she looked forward to it. She said that discovering the remains of an extra terrestrial civilisation was truly exciting but she was already missing the creature comforts of home. Kevin seconded her sentiments and added that he especially missed freshly cooked pizza with garlic bread. Melicia signed off by reminding him that the full impact of the storm would be upon them within three hours.

"You don't have to remind us of that, honey!" Kevin answered. "We are already feeling its approach."

Natasha stood by the urn drinking coffee. Although she didn't voice her concerns, the sight of Dmitri and Lee disturbed her. Part of her psychic sensitivity extended to seeing auras around people. By the colour of the aura she was often able to formulate accurate impressions about a person's personality and character. She had got used to seeing the normal pink and light green and orange hues in the energy fields around her friends. From time to time these hues would change to a golden yellow or lilac colour, all of which indicated perfectly normal well-balanced personalities. Indeed these were the colours that used to show in the auras of the two men the last time they were together. However, since that time something had changed. When she looked at the two men now all she saw was a horrid dark brownish black coloration that was more akin to a ghastly shadow than a healthy human aura. It caused mild nausea to arise within her. In the interval between them being left at the skyscrapers and their arrival here something had changed and she did not know what. Yet she said nothing for fear of alarming her friends unnecessarily. It could be that she was mistaken and simply confusing a tired and weary human for something more sinister and yet, considering the isolated and precarious situation they were in on this mission, she couldn't afford to rule anything out. She resolved to keep a close eye on them.

12

It took three hours for the camp to be re-erected. By that time darkness had descended and the shadow of the approaching storm had already begun to encroach upon their domain, raising small dust-balls at their feet. By now the familiar cold of the Martian night had begun to be felt and its chilly bite was only marginally kept at bay by the thermal suits the astronauts wore. Despite the cold and rapidly closing tempest they were not quite ready to retire for the night and wished to discuss their day's work before going to sleep. All gathered around the large thermal lamp in the centre of the camp. They ravenously devoured their supper and drank loads of coffee while they talked.

"There's plenty of architectural evidence but, apart from the mosaics and the metal plates upon the pyramids, there is not much in the way of lifestyle evidence," Ilya said. "I couldn't find a single piece of furniture, a picture or painting or even one of those cars Mary talked about. It's as if the inhabitants of this place suddenly packed their belongings and left, leaving next to nothing behind them. What could have caused such a huge and sudden exodus?"

"Don't underestimate our discoveries to date," Josh replied. "Those mosaics you discovered are priceless. I'm sure the scientists back home will be able to extract an enormous amount of knowledge from them. Furthermore, I believe it will only be a matter of time before that script on the pyramids is translated and then we will know what they were constructed for. Dmitri and Lee, I would be greatly interested in what you have to say about those skyscrapers."

The two men had been content to hover on the fringe of the gathering, listening to the others talk. Josh's question seemed to startle them. When the full attention of the others came to rest upon them, in anticipation of their reply, their sense of unease increased and they began to fidget nervously. Dmitri shrugged his shoulders, saying that compared to what the others had discovered here their findings were insignificant and warranted no special attention. Kevin implored them to tell more and Lee remarked that the skyscrapers were simply massive stone blocks which had been used, according to a theory that they had formulated, to serve some kind of symbolic purpose. When Mary asked what that purpose might have been, Dmitri responded they had not been able to determine that yet and they would have to return to make further tests, adding that was the reason they had to be alone to discuss their work as they did not wish to give their findings until their work had been properly completed. The others happily accepted this explanation and left the two men alone. All except Natasha. Her sharp black eyes were looking at the two men in an intensely suspicious manner. She could not put her finger on it but she felt there was something drastically wrong.

The Russian's psychic sensitivities were in a state of turmoil. To all intents and purposes the men she was looking at were Lee and Dmitri. Yet every fibre in her body told her that they were not. A feeling of deep sadness descended upon her heart and yet she could not account for it in any rational or logical manner. The feeling that she had just lost two dearly beloved friends caused a heaviness of spirit and mind, but why should she feel that way? After all, her two friends were standing right in front of her. They looked like her two friends. They were obviously well and alive. Yet her inner senses told her there was something wrong. Wanting to speak out she found she could not because the rational part of her brain told her not to be so silly. The rational part of her mind told her to accept the evidence of her physical senses, the evidence visible to her eyes and ears that Lee and Dmitri were both well and alive and so very obviously in her presence.

The other team members were oblivious to the silent inner battle that raged within Natasha as they conversed with the two men. She watched the way Lee was looking at Lorna's long blonde hair. It was a look she had never seen before in Lee, a look in which lust and covetousness mingled in equal proportions. Natasha noticed too that Kevin had become aware of the lustful manner in which Lee was viewing Lorna and, almost as an automatic reflex, stepped protectively closer to Lorna and threw a quick and angry glance at Lee. The ability to sense the truth about situations that were not as they appeared was Natasha's particular psychic skill. Mary did not appear to sense anything out of the ordinary judging by the free and easy way she talked to the two men. Psychic abilities obviously came in different forms and guises and each individual who possessed them displayed different aspects of them.

Mary reiterated, for the benefit of Dmitri and Lee, her vision at the pit and her conviction that it used to be a gladiatorial arena. Unexpectedly this remark brought a strange reaction. Suddenly the almost studied indifference in the expressions of the two men gave way to mild surprise. The look in their eyes said 'how could you possibly know that.' Dmitri pressed her for more information and asked her how she arrived at such a conclusion. Mary explained that she had had a vision of the Martian past where she saw men fighting a terrible monster inside the pit. She described the creature and the way the gladiators were dressed. Mary gave a detailed description of the scene she saw, the attire of the spectators and the surrounding countryside. Lee and Dmitri listened with keen interest as if the story she was relating stirred something inside them. Her descriptions seemed to captivate them and they looked at each other as if to say that they were in possession of knowledge that could only be known and shared by them.

"This seems to interest you," Josh said. He had noticed the changed look on their faces.

"I am most impressed by the sheer power of Mary's imagination, that's all," Dmitri replied dismissively.

Lorna explained that she and Yuri had spent the day studying the pyramids and the energy source. The pyramids were simply smaller versions of the ones they had discovered earlier, with one sole exception, that being the one with the mysterious energy source beneath it. She explained that it lay at a depth of nearly a mile below the pyramid and that it was impossible for them to gain access to it with the equipment and time restrictions of this particular mission. She said that future missions returning with the suitable heavy equipment might have a better chance. When questioned about the nature of the energy source Yuri explained that it was an exceptionally powerful and intense form of electromagnetism. More than that he could not say.

"Yes, we are impressed by what you have been able to discover here," Dmitri said in a slow measured tone of voice. "Please do carry on. I find it fascinating."

"We detected traces of electromagnetism in those black metallic pathways," Josh said. "Could there be a connection between that and the energy source beneath the pyramid?"

"Maybe," answered Yuri, "however, the energy source for the pathways seems to originate directly from the core of the planet. The energy below the pyramid is localised within one specific area. That indicates to me that it is contained within something. What that might be we can't say for sure yet. The most intriguing aspect is that it is encased within a metallic structure of some sort. That raises the possibility that it might be an artificially constructed object, whatever it is."

"You with the long blonde hair," Lee addressed his remark to Lorna. "What is your opinion?"

Lorna was puzzled and disturbed by this strange and uncharacteristic remark from Lee. The disconcerting expression on his face scared her. A cruel, mocking gaze had descended upon him and Lorna did not like it in the least bit. Turning to face Lee squarely in the face, she returned a strong defiant glare. It was apparent to all she deeply resented Lee's attitude and tone of voice.

"I don't know what's got into you Lee," she said firmly. "Why the hell are you addressing me in that strange manner? You're acting as if you're seeing me for the first time and I don't like that leering look in your eyes either."

"I suggest you watch your mouth mister!" Kevin said with tightly subdued anger. "If you talk to Lorna like that again I'll tear you apart."

Lee simply fell silent and said nothing further. Josh noticed this exchange and cast a wary glance over at Lee. The others too looked warily at him. Yuri in particular seemed to take great offence at this remark. Through working closely with Lorna he had built up a special rapport with her and he especially did not like the covetous way Lee viewed her. It caused strong emotions to arise within him.

"I suggest you take more care in what you say," Yuri angrily said to Lee. "I've always looked upon you as a good friend but if you carry on acting the way you are that will all change. You'd better show more respect towards Lorna. I too have noticed the way you have been looking at her recently. No woman should have to put up with behaviour like that. Are you sure nothing happened at the skyscrapers? You certainly have been acting strangely since you got back."

"Come, come, gentlemen! There's no need for this," Dmitri interrupted, "Lee's tiredness is simply affecting the way he thinks and acts. He'll be fine in the morning once he's had some sleep, and so will I. There really is nothing to worry about. Lee, apologise to Lorna and everybody else for your strange, erratic behaviour. I know you're tired and greatly stressed but there's no need to behave like that."

Lee looked up and glared at everyone around him. Although his mouth issued a verbal apology his eyes were not sorry. Ilya commented upon the need to maintain harmony and get the mission completed successfully. Kevin added that the mission had been such an outstanding success so far that it would be sheer folly to let petty bickering and rivalry spoil things now, especially now that they were so close to going home. Josh backed Kevin up vigorously and said he would not tolerate any further displays of antisocial behaviour from anyone. He then asked Natasha to relate what she had discovered.

Natasha spoke about her day's work, deciding to keep quiet about her inner unease for the time being. She explained that she had spent her time exploring the river bed and the oval shaped buildings plus some of the large mansion-type structures. She was able to provide a detailed architectural description of their construction but little evidence of the kind of lifestyles their former inhabitants pursued. For a split second she noticed a malicious glint in Dmitri's eyes which stopped her in mid sentence. She returned his glance with a bold stare. Waves of hatred shot forth from his mind and struck her but Natasha deflected them with a mental shield she had constructed by visualising a protective blanket of white light around her. This seemed to provide only minimal protection as the energy emanating from Dmitri's mind was exceedingly strong. The impression she had was that she had just encountered an alien mind that possessed psychic powers infinitely greater than hers and, furthermore, this alien knew about her inner thoughts and doubts and warned her not to divulge anything. Quiet indignation arose within her and she resolved not to submit to this telepathic intimidation.

"Red sandstone seems to be the most popular material used in the construction of most buildings," Natasha continued with a silent declaration of fierce defiance that refused to be bowed. "The state of workmanship is excellent. It would have to be considering the excellent state of preservation they are in even after all this time. Of course, the lack of dampness caused by the absence of water and the sheer cold of the environment would tend to help in their preservation. Much like those mammoths unearthed from the Siberian tundra. It's such a shame we can't find any organic remains. This whole planet is a gigantic refrigerator. If there were any organic remains such as frozen carcasses they would be in an excellent state of preservation. It would be a dream come true if I could unearth a frozen prehistoric Martian creature. It just puzzles me why there is no trace of organic life. The fact that this city exists proves that at one time it must have been here."

"I am curious as to why there are no artefacts left over from the past," Lorna said in exasperation.

"I have a theory which might explain that. The bombardment I saw in the dream pretty much destroyed everything," Mary said. "It's a miracle that these buildings are still standing. In my dream I can recall the inhabitants of the city being vaporised by the deadly rays. I'm certain the same thing happened to all their personal belongings. It was an extremely thorough operation. It's a miracle these buildings are still standing. I don't know why they weren't destroyed with all the others."

"I think the answer to that lies in their position," said Natasha. "If you look carefully you'll see these particular buildings are all nestled at the very edge of the mountain range. The mountains also shielded them from our prying eyes. If we had not made the effort of travelling here, this city would have remained hidden from us. When the bombardment started they were afforded a certain amount of protection. Fortunately for us they managed to survive. Otherwise we would have found a completely empty planet."

"Any guesses about the role of those large pillared buildings?" asked Josh.

"I would say they served a spiritual purpose of some kind. They may have been temples," replied Natasha.

"I wish there was some way of getting beneath that pyramid and finding out what that energy source is," Ilya said as he drank some coffee.

"So would I," Josh affirmed. "As Lorna has just said, we just don't have the equipment or the time to start excavating. We only have another three days before we return to the Ares and start our homeward journey. I want the remainder of our time here spent documenting and recording every single piece of data about everything we've discovered here. That is now our top priority. The excavation of whatever is underneath the pyramid will have to wait until a better equipped mission gets here. The more knowledge we can gather now the better prepared will be the missions that follow us. I'm sure that once the people on Earth hear about all that we've discovered, the governments of earth will be tripping over themselves trying to be the first to get back here. There will be no shortage of financial resources allocated to Martian exploration, I can assure you of that."

"I guess you're right," sighed Ilya in resignation. "Nevertheless I really would have loved to find out what is under there. We're so close and yet so far. How about an underground explosion? What have we got to lose? In that way we can see what's inside the pyramid and be able to get at what's underneath it."

"Oh, you don't want to touch that pyramid," Lee blurted out.

This unexpected remark brought proceedings to an abrupt halt. When asked what he meant by it Lee simply shrugged his shoulders and dismissed it as another one of those slips of the tongue he was famous for. This time, however, Josh would not let the matter die down so easily. Josh insisted that if Lee knew anything at all he must share it with the others, further adding that this was not a request but an order. Again Lee tried to dismiss the whole affair by saying it was only a careless and thoughtless remark and that he was not in possession of any secret knowledge. Lee kept his mouth stubbornly shut and Dmitri leapt to his defence by saying that everyone seemed to be picking on them since they returned from the skyscrapers and that it was totally unjustifiable, and that he and Lee were not hiding anything from anyone. After a few tense moments Josh let the matter go. Nevertheless, the look Josh gave Lee indicated that he was not satisfied with Lee's response and that serious misgivings were beginning to arise within him.

"I don't know what's got into you two," said Josh as he scrutinised the two men. "You're acting very strangely since you got back from the skyscrapers. Are you sure there's not something you're not telling us?"

"Of course not!" Dmitri said.

The idea of an explosion was dismissed as being impractical and dangerous as it would destroy the pyramid as well. The Earth authorities would never forgive them if they needlessly damaged an alien artefact.

The storm was now upon them. Swirls of dust began to rise at their feet and the howling of the wind grew ever louder. Lee and Dmitri went into their small tent whilst the others retired to the main tent. The occupants of the main tent lay on their beds. They were exhausted and desperately needed the sleep yet it would not come. The sheer amount of adrenalin pumping through their veins meant that sleep would not come easily. Their minds were ablaze with a thousand questions, questions for which there were no easy answers. However, from the occupants of the small tent sleep kept a savage and wary distance.

13

In their separate tent Lee and Dmitri sat in silence. Their senses were fully alert and not an iota of fatigue infected their bodies. They listened to the howling of the wind as it buffeted their tent. The plastic flaps on the outside of the tent blew fiercely and noisily as the wind shook them mercilessly. They heard the sound of equipment falling off the table but it caused them no concern. The fury of the elements did not trouble them in the least. On the contrary, it was a welcome symphony of sound that was lapped up with ardour. They savoured every second of it. Indeed, the ferocity of the Martian elements rekindled feelings of familiarity and joyous celebration.

"These humans have discovered that there is something beneath that pyramid," Dmitri said to Lee. "But we don't have to worry. They have no way of getting to it and can only guess at what it is. They have not even been able to translate the writing on the metal plates. That is most fortunate for us. It would complicate matters greatly if they realised what was below the pyramid. As things stand now we can afford to relax and bide our time a little bit. We shall use it to study these beings carefully before we act."

"It has been so long since I have savoured the fury of a Martian storm," Lee sighed deeply. "I had forgotten how wonderful it is. It is such a shame that these storms have been shorn of their water. The rainstorms of old were refreshing as well as humbling in their power. I longingly recall how they used to churn the oceans and seas of our world into wild tempestuous storms that used to lash the land mercilessly. All that is left now is a wind that cries a lonely and woeful lament. A wind that cries forlornly for the return of the days of old Mars."

"Those days are gone forever. Yes... those cruel Ilaks did a good job of destroying our planet," retorted Dmitri. "Damn them, wherever they are. Well, at the very least we can say that they did destroy our cursed gaolers. What a wonderful irony that our cursed gaolers, the sanctimonious and self righteous Martians, are all dead while we Toles are now on the threshold of a new life. These earthlings haven't got a clue what we have in store for them and their world. They should never have come here in the first place but their folly will be our liberation. Our old homes on Phobos and Deimos are destroyed. The Ilaks did that as a goodbye gesture. Our ancient worlds have been reduced to a state infinitely poorer than Mars itself. At least this planet is still structurally intact even though all the life has gone. Our worlds have been reduced to nothing but pieces of lifeless truncated rock held in place by the gravity of the former home of our bitter enemies. What a terrible irony. But one that will not matter much longer. These foolish aliens will provide us with a way out. A new home awaits us on Earth but you must be careful in what you say."

"What do you mean by that remark?" Lee asked angrily.

"Already thrice today you have made stupid and careless remarks that have aroused the suspicions of the aliens," Dmitri hissed back. "Their leader in particular, the one who calls himself Josh, is beginning to suspect that something is not quite right. Not only that, but one of the females, the one who calls herself Natasha, is aware of our presence. At the moment she can't prove anything but you must be careful lest you arouse their suspicions too far. Your careless remarks are making Josh and the others anxious. We must bide our time. There is still a lot we have to learn about these beings before we can advance to the second phase of our plan. We don't want our plans jeopardised by the humans becoming aware of our presence too soon. In future the less said the better. Simply perform your duties as requested and bring no undue attention to yourself. At the same time be extremely observant and learn as much as you can. In three days they will depart and we must be ready by then. Is that understood?"

"Yes, I apologise for my ineptitude but it's these human bodies," replied Lee. "They take some getting used to. I am having difficulty harmonising the action of the vocal chords with the thought processor in their primitive brains. They are very different from our own bodies which we used to inhabit thousands of millennia ago. The structure of the mind of these beings is a lot more rigid than our own. Their logical and rationalisation aspects have been inordinately developed at the expense of their intuitive powers, which is a Tole speciality. I need time to adjust but don't worry, from now on I'll keep my mouth shut. You seem to have adjusted to your host organism much quicker than I."

"Yes, I always was more intelligent than you and the passing of thousands of years has not made any difference."

"You are still as arrogant as ever," Lee hissed back. "Take care lest you underestimate these beings. I sense the two females have remarkably well developed intuitive powers. I noticed the one with the black eyes watching us extremely closely. Do you really think she suspects something?"

"I know she does!" Dmitri replied. "But she won't have enough time to do anything about it. These humans are on our world now. They are millions of miles away from any others of their kind. They are completely at our mercy. Besides, if she becomes too troublesome I will simply cause a breakdown in the primitive planetary conditioning process that enables these bodies to survive on our world and that will be the end of the matter."

"That Lorna intrigues me greatly," said Lee. "Her hair reminds me of our old foes except that it is of a different colour. She has an extremely pleasing form. If there are more like her on her world we shall indeed have a great deal of pleasure."

14

The wind howled furiously and swept up a violent dust storm which threatened to uproot the main tent. Inside the humans lay on their beds but sleep simply refused to visit them. In the midst of an onslaught by the raw fury of the wild elements of Martian nature the humans realised how alone they really were on this planet. Outside was an unwelcoming planet that offered no warmth or affection, only hostility and a callous indifference. The very thought that they were the only humans on an entire planet almost the same size as Earth was truly daunting. They felt alone and scared, the sense of isolation and dread being heightened by the fact that the nearest humans were millions of miles away across an expanse of desolate space. It was not as if they could pack their bags and pop on board an aeroplane and arrive back home in a couple of hours, something they had so taken for granted back home.

It was at moments like this they questioned why they really volunteered for missions such as this. On Earth it all sounded so very romantic and adventurous. The idea of travelling across space to another planet was enchanting in its magnificent romanticism. Whilst no one regretted making the journey, for it was truly a life-altering experience that would leave them forever changed for the better, there was now an awareness of another perspective. Once upon the planet, the romance is replaced by the desolate reality of an apparently lifeless world devoid of any beauty or warmth or any of the creature comforts humans so take for granted on Earth. The sense of adventure becomes tinged with the melancholy inspired by the extreme isolation of their situation and the hostility of the elements. The sheer distances involved completely overthrow all normal time-space reference points and result in a state of mental disorientation which only the very toughest humans can withstand.

The only security, comfort and solace they had was each in other's company, and on Mars that was a commodity far more precious than it could ever be on Earth.

"What's the matter with Lee and Dmitri?" asked Mary. "They're acting rather strangely. They appear cold and distant. Not like the dear friends we all know and love. It's beginning to spook me a little bit."

"You've noticed as well, have you," replied Josh. "It first struck me when they arrived at this city. I asked them a question and they just looked at me with a strange vacant expression on their faces. I put it down to tiredness and thought no more of it. But those strange remarks made by Lee, and the way Dmitri has become so protective of him, have got me worried. Perhaps there is something happening we're not aware of. If there is we better become aware of it right away. Our own lives could be at risk."

"Lee is beginning to make me nervous," Lorna said anxiously. "More than once I've noticed him looking at me in a very unsettling manner."

"Yes, I've noticed that too," Kevin said angrily. "Don't you worry about a thing Lorna. If he gives you any more trouble just let me know immediately."

"Don't worry, Lorna. We won't let anything happen to you," added Josh.

"I can certainly second that emotion!" declared Kevin.

"Could it be they've contracted some kind of Martian illness?" suggested Mary anxiously. "We know next to nothing about the effects of the Martian environment upon the human physiology. Although there are no bacteria or viruses on Mars, sickness may be caused by unknown factors within the environment that we're not aware of. Or perhaps the conditioning process has side effects we're not aware of?"

"That's a possibility but we have no proof," Josh reflected. "Besides, they look well enough physically. It's just their altered behaviour that's giving cause for concern, and so far they haven't really done anything dangerous or life threatening. I mean I can't condemn them simply for displaying small signs of unsocial behaviour, no matter how uncomfortable it may be for Lorna to be at the receiving end of it. Maybe Lee's always had strong feelings for Lorna but up until now he's suppressed them."

"I wish he'd keep them suppressed!" Lorna exclaimed. "That's the last thing I need on this trip, a lustful astronaut!"

"I think we might all be over-reacting," Yuri countered. "I mean we're all feeling fine and there's no sign that the conditioning process is in any way impaired. It's just those two who are acting strangely. If you ask me I simply put it down to stress. They can't withstand the mental pressure of being upon Mars and they're beginning to crack. Fortunately we're only here for a short time and I think we will be able to stave off any excessive deterioration in their condition. I would be more worried if this was a long term mission extending over a period of a couple of months. I say just ignore them and carry on with our work. In a few days we go back home and onboard the Ares they will revert back to their normal cheerful selves again."

"Perhaps, but I suggest we keep a close eye on those two," said Natasha. "I didn't want to say anything before out of fear of causing unnecessary alarm but now I feel I must speak out. Those two have not been the same since they arrived back from the skyscrapers. Their energy fields have altered drastically. That's the first thing I noticed about them and I've got a very bad feeling about them."

"Now you are scaring me!" Kevin exclaimed. "What do you mean by that? We are such a closely knit team here that if something happens to even one of us all are affected. In our peculiar circumstances of such extreme isolation and inter-dependency we simply can't afford any breakdown of harmony amongst us. It could have fatal consequences. If you think there is something wrong you had better tell us straight away."

"I can't say anything for certain at the moment," Natasha replied. "But when I look at them I don't see Lee and Dmitri any more. Sure, the bodies are the same, but something inside them has changed. Their energy fields have changed from light pink, which is what it used to be before, to a dark ugly brown. It's as if something has driven out Lee and Dmitri and planted itself within their bodies."

"Are you saying they're possessed?" Kevin asked in horror.

"I'm certain of it," Natasha replied. "I've already had a brief telepathic encounter with Dmitri and it wasn't Dmitri I encountered in that mind. It was something else more powerful, even deadly."

"Oh come on, spare me this nonsense!" Yuri cried out. "Natasha doesn't know anything for sure. All she is doing is speculating. I feel we should give them the benefit of the doubt. No harm has been done to anyone. This mission has progressed well and very soon we shall leave. Where is all this morbid nonsensical talk coming from? Natasha, I suggest you keep your mouth shut and let us carry on with our work. You want to believe in all this psychic rubbish... fine! But please don't try to infect our minds with your insidious fear-filled rubbish. I for one stand wholeheartedly by Dmitri and Lee and will not support anything that even looks like a witch hunt! Don't forget I've known Dmitri for nearly thirty years. I would have noticed if there was something wrong."

"There's no harm in keeping a close watch on them just in case, is there?" Natasha retorted quietly. "In our precarious situation on this planet we can't afford to take any chances. What if I'm right and they are possessed by hostile entities? We could be in grave danger. Let's not get too complacent and careless. All I am saying is that we should be open to the possibility and take sensible precautions. Both Mary and I have had experiences that confirm, as far as we're concerned, that there is a form of life on Mars. Since we know next to nothing about its true nature, or even if there are other lifeforms that we're as yet unaware of, I think it would be very wise to keep an open mind and make contingency plans. What have we got to lose?"

"Good idea," said Josh. "I am not going to jump to any premature conclusions. I agree with Yuri, we should give them the benefit of the doubt, but at the same time I don't want to take any chances with the safety of this team. I'm not saying I agree with Natasha but, just in case there is even a shred of truth in what Natasha says, I'm going to take precautions. Ilya, I'm going to assign a special mission to you. For the duration of our stay you will keep a close watch on them. Don't be too obvious about it but note everything they do and if anything in the least unusual happens let me know immediately. Is that understood, Ilya?"

Ilya replied emphatically that it was. Natasha then suggested that one of them should visit the skyscraper structures the two men had been studying prior to coming here. She felt certain that their strange behaviour was linked to them since they were perfectly fine back at the old campsite. Something might have happened to the men at the site of the skyscrapers and they should be checked out. If anything unusual was found it should be reported back immediately. This was

responsibility of looking after him to ensure there are no more unpleasant incidents. Please try not to be too hard on him."

Josh watched carefully as the two men walked to the table and began to analyse the rock and soil samples. This experience had shaken Josh and the others. Josh thought long and hard. It was his responsibility to safeguard the people on his mission. Things had taken an unexpected and inexplicable turn for the worse. The fact that they were on a planet millions of miles away from any possible help or assistance made it seem much worse. If this had happened on Earth there were security and police agencies that could assist. Here on Mars they were totally alone and completely dependent upon each other. If even one link in that chain of dependency broke down the safety and welfare of the whole group could be imperilled. He decided there and then to abort the mission and return to the Ares.

"The situation has become untenable," Josh said as he turned to face Kevin and Lorna. "I am going to abort the mission. This is a totally unprecedented and scary situation and I'm not sure how to deal with it effectively. There is now no doubt in my mind that we've got two aliens in our presence. Those two men you see sitting over there are not Lee and Dmitri. I have absolutely no doubt about that now. They are two aliens who have taken over their bodies. I am certain they mean us harm but are not as yet revealing their true intentions. Our problem is compounded by the fact that we know nothing about the nature of these aliens and what kind of powers and abilities they possess. They are simply biding their time and the longer we stay here the more at their mercy we become. We must act now."

"What shall we do?" Lorna asked anxiously.

"The mission is now ended," Josh declared. "Kevin, contact Melicia to advise her that we are returning a day ahead of schedule and get her to prepare for our return. Then go to the other team members and tell them to start packing up immediately. I want those transporters loaded up and ready to depart within three hours. Just take essential supplies and equipment, don't bother with the tents. Lorna, you help Kevin. Do not under any circumstances give in to fear. Our trust in God will see us through, I know it. Only fear can defeat us, nothing else. Do not talk to those two men. Leave that to me and Natasha. I will go and seek her out. If anyone has any chance of combating those two it's her."

The two men sitting at the table were engaged in a telepathic conversation. They had picked up the thoughts of the humans and knew everything they planned to do. They decided they could wait no longer. The second phase of their operation would have to be put into immediate effect.

17

Natasha was working in one of the larger domed buildings. The interior was spacious with a faded blue domed ceiling and a smooth black marble floor. The walls were cracked but still intact. The only sign that people once lived here were two metallic plates with that untranslatable Martian script. She passed the universal translator over the passage but again it gave a negative reply. In exasperation she slumped down onto the floor and sat cross legged as she surveyed the interior.

In truth, however, her mind was not focused on her work any more. Lee and Dmitri occupied her thoughts constantly. She knew now that two dangerous aliens occupied their bodies. She knew that both of her dear friends were now gone forever and that these aliens had killed her dear friend Ilya. Anger and rage burned within her. Shutting her eyes she began to contemplate the matter, trusting that somehow she would be able to make contact with the spiritual power that she knew resided within her: a power which she also knew could surmount all obstacles. From deep within the innermost chambers of her consciousness came the image of a tall long-haired man. This figure walked onto the inner screen of her mind and conveyed a message to her.

"Fear is your greatest enemy," the figure said and promptly vanished.

Natasha opened her eyes in surprise. Who the figure was she did not know except that he looked like the description Mary gave of the figure she claimed to see. Then it clicked in her mind that the figure she had seen was identical with the being she encountered telepathically earlier on at the Face. This experience helped to reassure her. It made her feel that they were not alone upon an hostile planet, that there might be a possible source of aid. This inner space encounter had helped to calm her mind and give her a boost in confidence. She knew she had to trust in the power of God and in her own internal power. She thought of ways in which she could combat the aliens whom she knew had taken over the bodies of the two men.

Intuitively she knew they were faced with a case of hostile possession. The aliens she was dealing with here were of a psychic nature. If they had been organic they would have been detected long ago. Her biggest disadvantage was that she knew nothing about the nature of these entities except that they were hostile and very powerful. She surmised that they wanted to take over the rest of the crew and were simply biding their time. Racking her brains in an attempt to find a solution she realised the sheer hopelessness of their situation. Against human spirits she might have had a chance but against alien ones possessed of infinitely more power she did not stand a chance. The best thing for them to do would be to leave Mars immediately and return home. She decided she would implore Josh to abort the mission straight away and leave before it was too late. Mars should then be quarantined until more could be found out about the aliens and ways of defeating them developed. As she hurriedly got to her feet something unexpectedly caught her attention.

Out of the corner of her eye she thought she saw a shadow. When she looked there was nothing there. She turned to head towards the exit when the shadow reappeared. This time she did not look at it directly and pretended to survey the side wall with the metallic plates, but all the time she was fully aware of the presence of something in the room with her. The shadow began to take on more depth and eventually materialised into a definite form. When she looked this time she saw clearly what was standing there. A man over seven feet tall with purple skin and long red hair. The man looked at her with intense purple eyes that were neither malevolent nor friendly. Although shocked at the sudden appearance of this entity Natasha was not afraid. Her training had taught her how to keep her fear at bay when confronted by a psychic apparition.

"Who or what are you?" she exclaimed in shock. "Are you the alien who has taken over Lee and Dmitri and killed Ilya?"

The figure did not answer. It simply watched with an unnervingly steady gaze. Then Natasha recalled that this was the person who had just appeared to her in her vision and conveyed the telepathic message. Suddenly she felt a feeling of warmth and reassurance come over her. She intuitively realised that this being was not malevolent and was not the same kind of alien that had taken over her friends.

"Leave this place immediately," the figure finally spoke. "You are in great danger. You have entered a world which, whilst not posing any physical danger, is certainly full of psychic danger. Your race is not yet fully equipped to deal with such matters. You are an exception as is one other woman on this mission but your powers are still embryonic compared to the powers possessed by the forces that lurk on this world. When you entered this planet you disrupted the aura of protection which I have been able to generate and maintain for almost a million years. Now the foolhardiness of a couple of your friends has released terrible forces. I sincerely hope they do not overspill the confines of this world. For that is what they intend to do and it would be a terrible thing if they succeeded. Leave now, I say. The only help I can give is the knowledge I have already imparted to you. Keep fear at bay and you will stand a better chance of surviving."

"I have already come to the same conclusion myself," she replied excitedly. "I was on my way to ask my mission commander to abort the mission and leave. We can't fight what we're up against, not here on Mars with our present level of understanding. But coming face to face with you is fantastic! It's our first real and tangible contact with a Martian. Are you an astral form or are you physical?"

"I am both and I am neither but that is of no consequence," replied the figure. "You are wasting time. Leave now."

"Who are you and why have you appeared to me now?" she said insistently.

"You ask me questions!" exclaimed the entity with mild irritation. "You who have intruded upon my world presume to ask me questions. I suggest you leave now. The longer you stay the less your chance of survival."

"We are on a peaceful scientific mission. We mean no one any harm," Natasha replied.

"I know," responded the entity. "However, the Toles intend you a great deal of harm. Already two of your party are possessed by them and they have killed a third, as you are already aware. I have been aware of your presence since your vessel entered the planetary aura of my world, which extends up to a distance of two thousand kilometres around this planet. It has been a very long time since this world has received visitors from another world. The last time it happened was nearly thirty thousand years ago when a group of aliens from another solar system came here to mine iron. Fortunately, they had the good sense not to tamper with these old monuments. I realised you and the one called Mary were the most psychically receptive. That's why I tried to contact you to warn you against staying here. Obviously I did not get the message through well enough. Leave now. The longer you stay the greater the chance of the rest of you being taken over."

"We humans don't scare that easily!" Natasha retorted. "Exploring the unknown always entails risk. Our race has never been scared of that risk. In fact we willingly take it in order to advance our knowledge and understanding of the universe around us. Mars is no exception. It doesn't matter if we all die. There will be other missions after us and eventually we shall overcome all obstacles that stand in our way, including these damned aliens who have killed my friends and taken over their bodies. I ask again: who are you and who or what are the Toles?"

"I like your spirit!" the figure answered. "You are an inquisitive race. Very well, if you must insist. I am Maran. I am the Watcher of Mars. It is my task to watch over Mars in its current planetary cycle. I am not allowed to intervene directly in the affairs of those who reside upon my world. However, I can, when the circumstances warrant it, indirectly intervene to assist those in need of help. That is why I tried to contact you earlier telepathically and am now making a personal appearance. It is not something I do often."

"Are you the one who appeared to Mary?" she asked.

"Yes, that was me," Maran replied. "I was curious to see at close hand what kind of people had visited my world. I realised you were from Earth. You probably are not aware of this but people from your world used to visit Mars regularly. But that is now forgotten history for most humans. Everything would have been fine if your friends had not released the Toles. They did it unwittingly in the interests of furthering science but they knew not what they were dealing with. Now it may be too late."

"What do you mean by that statement?" Natasha asked.

"Those towers you loathe so much held the Toles," Maran continued. "They are the hostile aliens you are facing. They are the ones who killed your friends and they mean to kill you as well. You intuitively sensed that there was something unpleasant inside them. That's why you all disliked them so much. However, your two friends were foolish enough to blow a hole in the side of one of the towers. That one single act of reckless disrespect released the Toles, and your friends paid dearly. Now the ramifications of their action threaten to overspill this world and reach yours. Millions could be affected. That is why I have taken this rare step of materialising in front of you, so that you can see that I am a real being, that I really do exist."

"Tell me more! I am fascinated by what you have to say," implored Natasha. She seemed momentarily to forget the danger she and her team were in. Meeting Maran felt like coming into contact with a semi-divine figure and it thrilled her senses more than the wildest roller-coaster ride ever could. She was absolutely mesmerised by what he had to say.

"Once I watched over a beautiful and thriving planet," Maran continued again. "Even people from the misty prehistory of your world used to visit Mars for trade purposes. The Atlanteans in particular were extremely impressed by our architecture and scientific knowledge. They took the designs back home and they became the prototypes of the later civilisations that followed after the destruction of Atlantis. But Mars suffered a terrible fate. The ruler of Mars unwisely offended a high-ranking member of the Galactic Council by daring to invade a planet under his protection in the Sirius solar system. So enraged was this being that it ordered the destruction of Mars. The Ilaks from the Orion constellation were charged with the destruction of Mars. When the Ilaks go to war their efficiency and savagery know no equal. They reduced this beautiful world to an empty shell. What you see now is what was left behind. A few paltry monuments and pyramids and the ruins of a once glorious city. Even to this day my heart grieves for this world and I must remain the Watcher of Mars until my term expires. That won't be for at least another ten millennia."

Maran went quiet for a while. His face took on the anguished look of a soul that was recalling painful memories from the past: memories that still retained the power to cause great pain after so many millennia had passed since the events took place. Natasha felt a sense of empathy for this being and had lost any fear that his sudden appearance had first caused. Maran looked up from the floor and started to speak again.

"There used to be two races on Mars. The Martians shared their world with the Toles who originated on the two worlds that orbit Mars. At one time they too were lush beautiful worlds. However, the Toles were a cruel and fierce people. For centuries they intermingled with the Martians on the pretext of conducting trade. They built cities of their own next to the native Martian settlements yet they did not intermingle to a great degree. They kept a cool and respectable distance which the Martians regarded as being a sign of their intrinsic arrogance. However, the Toles were good traders and had much to offer in terms of merchandise and technology and thus the Martians tolerated their presence. All the time the Toles were really trying to work out a way to take control of Mars. They stockpiled secret piles of weapons and their leaders drew up all kinds of ingenious plans for conquest. For a long time that was impossible due to the strength of the Martian civilisation. It was only when Mars was struck by a great natural cataclysm a million years ago that the Toles showed their true colours and attempted to take over the planet. However they overestimated the degree of damage done to the Martian civilisation by the earthquakes, volcanic eruptions and tidal waves and instead of achieving a swift stunning victory, as they had over-confidently expected, they instigated a centuries-long series of bitter civil wars. The last final battle depicted on the temple wall was the final defeat of the Toles. By way of punishment all surviving Toles had their life essences extracted and sealed within specially constructed prison towers. That's what those tall skyscraper structures near the Face are."

"No wonder I never liked them!" Natasha exclaimed.

"Yes," replied Maran. "The essences are immortal but cannot function without an organic host. Once they find a host they take over its body and mind. Your two friends have now been taken over by them. Although they look like your friends they are not. It is now a hostile Martian consciousness which occupies their form. There are many thousands more of them. The plan is to free all of them and get off this planet and travel to yours where they will take it over."

"Not if I can help it!" Natasha exploded angrily. "I would rather sacrifice my life and the lives of all the other crew members rather than see them use our bodies to get to Earth. There must be a way to stop them."

Maran was about to start talking again but Josh's shouting voice reached them and Maran disappeared. Natasha rushed towards him as he walked in through the entrance. Her greatly excited and nervous state caused him to be taken aback. A sense of feverish delirium seemed to envelop her and it shocked him. He asked if she was okay with a bewildered and concerned expression on his face.

"I'm fine, Josh!" Natasha replied in a state of great agitation. "I've got something to tell you."

"Me too," he said. "I'm aborting this mission right now. Start packing and be ready to leave as soon as possible."

"He was here, he was here!" Natasha exclaimed excitedly.

"What are you talking about?" Josh said.

"The Watcher of Mars was here. He's told me everything," Natasha exclaimed.

"Hang on, Natasha, you're not making any sense. Who's this watcher and what has he told you?"

"I don't have time to explain, just trust me," the Russian shouted. "I was going to suggest the same thing to you anyway. You've obviously picked up my thought waves. How are Lee and Dmitri behaving?"

"That's the reason I'm aborting the mission," said Josh. "Their behaviour, Lee in particular, is becoming more erratic and anti-social. Downright hostile, in fact. I'm rapidly losing control over them. I now fully believe what you said about the possibility of them being possessed by Martian spirits. Lee even challenged my command and made a threatening gesture. I've decided to cut short the mission and return to the Ares. Things have taken a very sinister turn and it's best we leave before it gets too late."

"That's an excellent idea," Natasha said hurriedly. "They have been taken over by the spirits of an old Martian race that used to live here. They are called Toles and they are hostile. They are raging with the fury of thousands of years of pent-up anger and hatred. Lee and Dmitri inadvertently released them by blowing a hole in the side of one of the towers. The fact that we sent Yuri to visit the towers, and he has still not returned, makes me suspect that he has fallen victim to the Toles as well. They plan to take us all over and get to earth where they will wreak havoc. We must act now!"

"What shall we do with Lee and Dmitri?" Josh asked.

"They are not Lee and Dmitri," Natasha replied coldly. "We must kill them. Our dear friends have long gone. All that remains are their bodies, empty shells which have been taken over by malevolent spirits from ancient Mars. They will do the same to us if we give them the chance. They must be destroyed now. Since we don't have any weapons I suggest blowing them up with the explosives that we have."

At first Josh was shocked by this idea. Then he remembered the cold evil look in their eyes whenever they now looked at him, and the menacing gesture that Lee had just made. He was the captain and he had to think of the safety of his crew. If he allowed his emotions and sentimental attachments to the memory of two friends who, as he was now increasingly forced to accept, were almost certainly dead to warp his judgement the consequences could be extremely severe. If his feelings for his old friends were allowed to cloud his objectivity, and as a result he made the wrong decision, he might end up sacrificing the lives of all his crew, including his own life. Far worse, the wrong decision on his part held the awful potential of leaving Earth vulnerable to the Toles. That prospect, more than anything else, terrified him. If what Natasha claimed was true, and his gut instincts told him it was, the people on earth would not stand a chance. They would be like sitting ducks waiting to be picked off by cruel and evil aliens. Yet the memories of the many pleasant associations he had had with his friends, going back many years, were strong and fought hard to sway his decision in their favour. He racked his brains in a desperate attempt to come to a decision. Space Academy never prepared him to deal with a contingency such as this.

"All right, let's do it. I have no choice," Josh said with a heavy heart. "The lives of too many people are at risk. I simply can't risk leaving the millions of humans on Earth, which include all our families and friends, exposed to the merciless designs of these fiendish Toles. For the sake of all mankind I must destroy them."

"You can oversee and direct the termination of the mission," Josh said to Natasha as they walked hurriedly back to the camp. "I will go directly to the transporter and get the explosive charge ready. I must catch them by surprise otherwise it will not work. Just make sure that all the others are as far away from Lee and Dmitri as possible. Once I've rigged up the bomb I will throw it at them and hope for the best. May God have mercy on my soul."

"He will, trust me," Natasha replied reassuringly.

However, Josh and Natasha walked into a nasty surprise when they reached the campsite. Kevin was lying unconscious on the ground. Lee was standing over him. Dmitri had all the other team members huddled into the corner of a rock face. Lorna and Mary were enclosed within a shimmering electronic forcefield which Dmitri was somehow emanating and controlling. The sight of his friends being held in such brutish captivity enraged Josh. He tried to rush

The spacecraft resumed its trek towards Earth. The two women looked back at Mars as it gradually faded into the distance. Mars had proved a greater adventure than anyone had ever expected. They looked forward to returning and finishing unfinished business.